Keenan's

This Is Memorial Device won the Collyer Bristow Award for Debut Fiction and was shortlisted for the 2017 Gordon Burn Prize.

His second novel, *For the Good Times,* won the 2019 Gordon Burn Prize.

Edna O'Brien described reading his third novel, *Xstabeth,* as "feel[ing] like being cut open to the accompanying sound of ecstatic music."

His most recent novel, *Monument Maker,* is due out from Europa in 2023. He lives in Glasgow, Scotland.

David Keenan

XSTABETH

Europa
editions

Europa Editions
1 Penn Plaza, Suite 6282
New York, N.Y. 10019
www.europaeditions.com
info@europaeditions.com

Library of Congress Cataloging in Publication Data is available
ISBN 978-1-60945-734-1

Keenan, David
Xstabeth

Book design by Emanuele Ragnisco
www.mekkanografici.com

Cover photo: Used with kind concession of the author

Prepress by Grafica Punto Print—Rome

Printed in Italy

For Xstabeth

David W. Keenan was a (non-political) writer, teacher and local historian (whose "great passion in life [*was*] literature and music, as well as the researching and publishing of the local history of his home town, St. Andrews, in Scotland"), who committed suicide by throwing himself from the top of the tower of St. Rule in the autumn of 1995.

In the early 1990s he ran a correspondence course that taught magick, tarot and bibliomancy via ethno-poetics and avant-garde literature, which was known as St. Rule's School for Immaculate Fools, or SR|SIF for short. It also had an inner order: Dx(e).

His articles for the *St. Andrews Oracle* were collected in a series of self-published pamphlets in the late 1980s entitled *St. Andrews Oracle Articles by David W. Keenan* as well as *A Book of Shadows by David W. Keenan*. They can often be found cheap in the little bookshop near the top of Market Street in the town.

Some of his most interesting articles include: "Xstabeth Isappearing," a revisiting of the tale of a ghost said to take the form of a "grey lady" who walked The Scores and plied her trade by the castle; "Wilson's Brewery," a self-explanatory rags-to-riches success story involving Aitcheson's (of Edinburgh) pale, export and strong ales; "Tobacconists of St. Andrews," a lament for the "general trend away from pipe smoking that occurred in the 1960s"; "Churches of Old St. Andrews," a lament; "The Heyday of Craigtoun Park," a lament; "Octogenarian Golfer Recalls Old St. Andrews," a lament; and "The Dutch Village," sadly, a lament.

He self-published one novel in his lifetime, 1992's *Xstabeth*, reissued here and updated with commentary, newly discovered, by students of SR|SIF, alongside assorted addenda.

David W. Keenan

XSTABETH

(ILLUMINATED EDITION WITH COMMENTARY)

Introductions in Xstabeth
by Ruth White (SR|SIF)

An introduction is quite the simplest thing. It is a moving from silence into speech, and shortly, back again. Introductions are made, daily. They can be advantageous, or, just as often, detrimental. Whether you read an introduction is one thing, whether you make one is another. I would say that the purpose of an introduction is to ease one in, which is why I often leave it to the last, so that I may, as I say, ease myself in *all over again*. The best introductions, then, in my view, or according to my view, which, as I have already stated, is backwards, would be a summation or, rather, an elaboration, of mood. Which is why I prefer to save them for last, through fear of the depths, I admit, through fear of getting too deep already, or too soon, because I prefer the gentle arc of a beach in the evening to a perilous drop from a clifftop in full sun.

When I was small and the trees were very high. This was in Russia. My dad was a musician. A famous musician. But he was friends with a musician who was even famouser. I went to his lecture. The famouser musician. He did a lecture. His speciality was moral philosophy. But in this lecture it was different. In this lecture he spoke against morals. I couldn't believe it. My teenage mind was like that. What. He said it was okay to be immoral. That's what he said. In so many words. Words like "permission," "authority," "refusal." "Autonomy." I remember that one. "Belief." That was still key. Funnily enough. Afterwards we went with him. My father and I. And we drank vodka. I know it's typical. But we also drank stout. Russian imperial stout 12 per cent. That's also typical. I asked him a question. I said to him you mentioned permission but who is asking permission and who is giving it. If you know what I mean. I just came right out with it. He said it was a good question. That's a good question. He said. He was from Moscow. Originally. Typical. Typical of intellectuals to come from Moscow. Or the Urals. I knew a few from the Urals but I was too nervous to approach them on the whole. This was

different. He was a musician. Somehow that made it
different. Softer. I pushed my point. I pursued my
question. But at first he just kept looking into thin air.
How can you just be bad. I wanted to say. But of course
that was illiterate to a Russian. So I phrased it a different
way. How can you give yourself permission. I said. I used
one of his words strategically. How can you give yourself
permission to perform acts that go against yourself
otherwise why do you need to give yourself permission to
do something if it comes naturally anyway. I said. That's a
good question. He said. He said it again. I began to realise
that a good question was something that would stop you
in your tracks. Well. He said. There are all sorts of things
that have given you permission that weren't you and that
you never knew you wanted to do anyway. I know in a way
that's elementary philosophy but at the time it really struck
me. Like what. I said. Well. He said. Do you think it is
beautiful to be on the beach at night beneath the stars.
This guy was from Moscow where a beach with stars is
more than a dream. Yes. I said. It's romantic. Who
doesn't. Especially in Moscow. All the time my father was
just observing me. He was seeing how I was doing up
against an intellectual who was famouser than him. What
if it's freezing cold at night. The intellectual musician
asked me. What if you are standing there shivering and in
the distance you can smell sewage. This is a Russian beach.
I said. For sure. It's still a beach under the stars. I said.
Nothing can change that. What if I told you someone was
murdered there. He said. I didn't see that coming. It's a
beach in the dark. He said. You know nothing.

* * *

I had an affair with the immoral musician. Who was famouser than my father. I say it was an affair. But I wasn't cheating on anyone. Neither was he. At first. But it was an affair because I had to hide it from my father. Who would have been jealous of the famouser musician who was having an affair though not really with his daughter. It started when he slipped his hand onto my leg on the first night. Which was the night after his talk. Which was the night of the beach in the dark. He slipped his hand onto my thigh. Which was bare and had goosebumps from the cold and from his touch. Which was sudden and exciting. But which didn't linger. Honey. He said. He called me honey. It's a big bad world out there. He said. Then he said something else. He said one never knows. I thought to myself what kind of a Russian speaks like Shakespeare. Like Dostoevsky. Surely. Like Tolstoy. Perhaps. Like Solzhenitsyn. No doubt. Plus. The famouser musician had a beard like old Solzhenitsyn too. Or was that Gogol. A beard where it just grew down from beneath the chin. I thought to myself. This could be an education. It was confusing how he said it though. I thought does he mean one never knows but two might know. Or that two together had a chance of finding out. Moscow intellectuals are as cryptic as ever. Even if they don't survive on black bread and water in a garret anymore. Then I thought. Does he mean that one never knows ever. And that it was even impossible to read his own intentions. For good or for worse. That gave me a thrill and scared me at the same time. A beach in the dark. I thought to myself. Who knows what has taken place. I was starting to come round to his way of thinking. It had only taken me half an hour. Then my father came back to the table and they began to talk about old times together. I felt excluded. Especially when they got really drunk and the famouser musician took out a penknife. He wanted to play the game that Russians love. Which despite what everyone says isn't Russian roulette. Most people in Russia can't afford a gun with bullets missing. Even though the black market is everywhere. No. It's five-finger fillet that the Russians love the best. Because everyone has a penknife. You spread your hand out on a table and then stab a knife quickly back and forth between your fingers. There's a reason why Russia has the least fingers. But the famouser musician had perfect hands. That's what I noticed. I thought we really don't know what is going on here. Either he was the best player of the game Russia has ever seen. Or he was bluffing and had never played it before. Which was unlikely with him being a famous musician and a moral philosopher and a drinker too. But when he asked my father to go first. When he asked my father to go first I got a terrible feeling. Like he wanted my father to stab himself right through the back of his palm and attach himself to the table. So that he could make off with his daughter. He looked at me for a second. Then he said. Let's see what the old man is made of. That only made things worse. Of course my father had his own penknife. A blue Swiss Army number. But he was so drunk that he opened it up

at the corkscrew and not at the blade. The famouser
musician laughed at my father. You old fool. He said.
We're trying to open your hand not a bottle. That gave
the game away right there. He did plan to have my father
stab himself. Though not really. It wasn't as if my father
was under his control. Besides. Everyone played this game
when they were drunk. That was normal. But I did
wonder how my father could mistake a twirly corkscrew
for a straight blade. He must be far gone. I thought. But
then I wanted to stick up for him. He's fucking with you.
I said. Just like that. I pretended that my father was acting
the goat. Stop fucking with him father. I said. I reached
out and closed the corkscrew and opened up the blade
which was inevitably rusty. Russian penknives tend to be
well loved. That's another thing. My father didn't
respond. I think he realised his mistake and was
becoming nervous. He put his hand on the table and he
placed the blade slowly and carefully between his thumb
and forefinger. Like he was lowering a crane into position.
He had one eye closed like he was painting a miniature
Madonna. Then he went for it and came out without a
nick. Then he looked at the famouser musician and he
took his penknife and threw it across the road and into
the river. But all the time he didn't take his eyes off the
famouser musician. A Russian throwing his penknife into
the river is the ultimate insult.

* * *

We had our own codes that we used. We had a system.

On a Sunday morning the famouser musician would call and let the phone ring three times. My father would play golf on a Sunday morning. Of course they play golf in Russia. What do you mean. Lee Trevino and Seve Balles-teros are like heroes there. And they all dream of one day travelling to St. Andrews and playing drunk on the Old Course.

He would call three times and then hang up. If the coast was clear I would call him back. What would we talk about? Philosophy mostly. He said I was an agnostic. Then a pessimist. Then a nihilist. I told him that really I was a romantic. He was trying to get to the bottom of me. I thought I was quite shallow. I hadn't read much philosophy. So I didn't really know what I was talking about. But then I realised that attractive young people are endlessly deep to older people. They are literally unfathomable. You're unfathomable Aneliya. The famouser musician would say to me. That's just the word he used. And then I thought no. It's just because I echo. It's just because I'm empty enough to echo. Sometimes it was awkward. Sometimes I had nothing to say and I would just hang on the line in silence. But then I learned that if I did that. If I did that he would fill the gap with compliments and echoes. He compared me to certain months. To the beauty of a wild mountain. I thought all mountains were wild. I thought that was normal. No. He said. Some mountains cannot be tamed. But most of them in the end can be conquered. It all went to my head. As you can imagine. I started seeing less of my friends. My good friends that were my own age. For instance Marja. Tiny Marja with the so cute buck teeth. I shunned her company. She would turn up at our door looking to go out and hunt for birds' eggs. But I would instruct my father to say that I wasn't in. Then I would watch her through the curtains from upstairs. She would turn and look up towards me. Towards my room. Where I was hidden behind the curtains. And her buck teeth would implore me not to give up on all of the fun we could have as young girls. She was like a poor little rabbit. But I told myself. I have the love of a man. I told myself. An immoral philosopher. Who needs little frightened rabbits. And my father downstairs. My father downstairs would be playing a Leonard Cohen song on the guitar. My mother had been taken from us long ago and he would play "Famous Blue Raincoat." And he would sing that line about taking the trouble from her eyes. And I would think to myself yes. Yes. I understand. An affair can do all of that. I felt so grown up and doomed and romantic and sad. I stared out of the window and saw Tiny Marja disappear like a speck of dust.

* * *

St. Peters is cold but it's nice where I'm living. That was a line that I could relate to. Your bitterest foe is dead now. My dad would sing. His voice would rise up from downstairs. I would imagine the famouser musician in his apartment. Alone or maybe even with a naked woman sitting on the edge of the bed. Maybe she was upset and sobbing quietly while the famouser musician slept. Or maybe they had just made love and she was going to the bathroom. Did you ever isappear. My dad would sing. His voice echoing up the stairs and right now echoing out of the past. And I never understood that line. I never knew what it meant to isappear. Later on I found out for myself. But then I imagined it to do with opening yourself up to the light. Leonard Cohen struck me as a very honest musician. That's what my father would say. Leonard Cohen has lived it. He would say. Then he would play another one. "Bird on the Wire." A song about trying to be free. This is raw emotion. My father would say. This is authentic. That was always the word he used. Do you understand that little one. He would call me little one when he was drunk but before he tipped over. Even though I was nineteen years old.

My father tried to make money as a musician. Even though he was past his prime. He put out some records that were a mix of cover versions and originals. But he was naive. That's why I still loved him. If you were to ask me for my single favourite quality. I would say naivety. He always had big plans. For instance. The tall trees that grew outside our window and that made me feel so small. He took four photographs of them. One in spring. One in summer. One in autumn. One in winter. Then he had them printed as a calendar. One photograph for every three months. One photograph for each of the seasons. He called it *The Changing Forest* and he tried to sell the idea. Of course no one was interested. It wasn't even a forest. But my father couldn't see that. He thought it was a great idea. He was excited about it. It made me cry every time I looked at the calendar. Which was quite a lot because it hung at the end of my bed for several years. And the pictures on the calendar matched the view outside my window. And of course made it more like a forest. A forest on an endless loop. Which of course is what all forests are. And what childhoods are too. When you're right in the middle of them. Or when you're looking back at them from way yonder. From afar.

My father was on TV. It was a comedy sketch show where they had guest slots. He sang one of his own songs. Everyone thought it was his big break. Then a comedian came on dressed like a bohemian and played a song that mocked men like my father and Leonard Cohen. He had a name that was an awful pun. He smoked a cigarette and his hair was all in his eyes. He almost bent double over his guitar. Like he was using his own belly button as a microphone. He sang words like "destitution" and "despair" and "it's so hard." Then he started singing things about Mama's money and about Papa's money. About how it ain't no good. Then he began howling about how he was fixing to die. And who shot out the lights. Who shot out the lights. Mama. He sang. Who turned down the sound. And of course the joke was that they faded him out and turned his sound off. My father stood up. On live television. And he applauded. He applauded the joke. Who is that man. He asked the presenter. Does he have any records out. My father launched into an impassioned rant on live TV. We need more of this kind. He said. This is the new man. He announced. Run a guitar string into a vein. He said. Play your songs washed in blood. That was when the comedy protest singer came back onstage. He pulled his wig off and revealed that he had been the co-presenter dressed up all the time. My father froze. He was furious and embarrassed. He had been made to look like a fool. But he was too naive even to pretend that he had just been playing along with the sketch. It was all too real. He stormed off the set. Everybody thought he was a joke from then on. Not me. Naivety gets me every time. Knowledge can be cynical. It just gets used to undermine things. Sarcasm and irony are horrible. But naivety is the deepest form of belief. It's closer to reality. To wonder. Plus it has more love in it.

* * *

On the phone to the famouser musician. I said to him. You need to practise a bit of naivety. Who have you been reading. He asked me. Nietzsche. I might have been. I said. I was too embarrassed to admit that I'd just come up with it out of my own head. Creative naivety. He said. Or was that Schopenhauer. It was one of those comedians. He said. I just sat there silent until I started echoing again. Listen. He said. Let me take you to the movies. My father would never let me out of his sight in the evenings. I told him. There's not much chance of that. But secretly I was dying to go. I had never been to the movies with a

man on my own yet. Here. He said. I have an idea. He
had an idea to get my dad a gig. To pull some strings and
get him a show. My dad hadn't played since the TV
comedy incident. No one would take him seriously. But
the famouser musician could get him a gig. Everybody
listened to him. Okay. I said. It's a deal. That way my
father could resurrect his career. Plus. I could get to see
what a date at the movies was all about. The famouser
musician called my father the next day. I could hear him
on the phone downstairs. At first he played it cool. I
heard him using the words "bastards" and "reprobates"
and "philistines" and "ironists." They don't deserve me.
He said. He was talking to himself really. Eventually he
agreed to do it. But there were conditions. No interviews.
He said. As if there would be any interviews. No support
act. He said. As if anyone was willing to support him. No
photographs. He said. As if anyone wanted to take his
picture. Plus. I play two sets of one hour each. As if
anyone would sit through one set. It broke my heart. I
knew my father had talent. I knew he had a special belief.
But I also knew that no one else cared. And of course. I
knew that he was only getting the gig so that his famouser
friend could sneak me away and have sex with me let's
face it in the back row of the cinema. Two sets. He
insisted. One originals. And one all Leonard Cohen
covers. Whatever you say. The famouser musician must
have said. Because my father hung up happy. He called
me from the bottom of the stairs. Little one. He said.
Little one they want me. He lifted me up. And I hugged
him. And I wrapped my legs around him. I imagined him

passing me over to the famouser musician in exactly the same position. Me clinging to him like a limpet. My father picking up his guitar and walking out of the door like a cowboy. But maybe that's just because of what happened next.

* * *

On the night of the show the famouser musician called my father. He apologised for not being able to come to the show himself. He said he had some hassle with a chick. Those were his exact words. I couldn't help but smirk. But then I felt bad. My father was annoyed. Jaco can't make it. He said. The famouser musician's nickname was Jaco. Damn it. My father said. I'm all on my own here. Jaco had my back. He said. I'll be out late. My father said. Don't wait up for me. I imagine there's going to be a bit of a do afterwards. He said. A bit of a do. That phrase really caught me when he said it. It still catches me now. I imagine there's going to be a bit of a do. I wished him well. Kill them stone dead. I said to my father. Murder them. And I really meant it. Have a ball. I said to him. Then I waited for the door to slam. Then I ran upstairs. And hand-washed my best panties. Which were black and which had a red love heart on the back. I put on my best nylons and my heels. I wore my hair up but with carefree strands hanging down. That way I looked like a seductive intellectual. In other words just his type. I put on red lipstick and smoky eyeshadow. I practised smoking a cigarette in front of the mirror. Making my mouth a perfect O. He rang the phone three times as was usual. I could see his car across the road. It was a gold Viva. He was wearing a pair of shades and his arm was dangling out of the driver's window. His dark hair was slicked back. I could almost smell him from there. That musky smell. He was tapping the sides of the car to the music. He was playing a cassette. It was a blues song. You know the one. Delia. Delia. How can it be. You say you love those ramblers but don't love me. I threw a black shawl over my shoulders. Then I swayed over to his car. Oh my. He said. When he looked at me. Oh wow. Oh baby. He said. And he got out and opened the passenger door for me. But before we drove off. Before we drove off he put his hand on my thigh. Just the way he had before. Only this time he used it to slide my dress up my legs a little bit. So that he could see my stocking tops.

* * *

The movie was a cowboy movie. That's why I mentioned cowboys earlier. I was surprised. I thought he would have taken me to a movie about suffering and loneliness. You don't get it. He said. I had expressed surprise about the cowboy movie. This is the final frontier. He said. Don't you know the difference between a wilderness and a garden. He asked me. It seemed like a boring difference whatever it was. The cowboy is the ultimate existentialist. He told me. He's no armchair philosopher. He said. He gets on his horse. He said. And he rides. What's he looking for. I asked him. Absolution. He said. But what about killing all those Indians. I asked him. We were at a stage in the movie where the Indians had been ambushed as they passed along a thin path between two high rocks. That's the point. He said. And he put his hand back on my thigh and hooked his little pinky beneath my stocking top. The point is that after all the thought and deliberation. After all the thought and deliberation he gets back in the saddle and does what is asked of him. I didn't see much thought and deliberation. I had to be honest. But perhaps that happened off-screen. After all that would be even more boring than a garden and a wilderness. But who asks it of him and what do they ask. I pressed the famouser musician. Who I might as well start calling Jaco like everyone else. Maybe I was trying his patience a little. Or maybe I seemed smart and unwilling to accept easy answers. Call it what you want. He said. Call it the word of God. Destiny. The heart. Fate. A calling. True will. Listen. He said. And he moved his hand up to just above my breasts and slipped it in between the buttons of my dress. Listen. He said. And he left it there as the Indians were massacred in the narrow pass.

* * *

Afterwards we went to a bar and the famouser musician started to get drunk. Vodka was in the picture. I had a pale ale 8 per cent and stared at him from behind the glass. He was becoming impassioned. I thanked him for getting a gig for my father. I told him it was a decent thing to do. But he just laughed. Your father is a terminal case. He said. I had no idea what he was getting at. He was really drunk by this point. At least my father believes in something. I went to say. But then I didn't. I remembered the beach in the dark and how no one really knows anything. I didn't want to make a fool of myself. Some people came past and patted Jaco on the shoulder and said congratulatory things to him. They didn't even notice me. I began to imagine that he was regularly seen with young girls gazing at him from behind their glass. I imagined what was going on in his head right then. For a moment I saw myself tied to a chair in nothing but my underwear. Wow. Did I just see a picture in his mind. I thought. Then he asked me if I had ever been to a strip club. I hadn't seen that in his mind. I lied and said yes. Yes. I said. Of course. But really I only knew them from videocassettes. I know a good one. He said. One where we will be made most welcome. By this point he could barely stand. I felt sorry for all the strippers up ahead. But somehow he was still attractive to me. Like a wild mountain. Maybe.

When the taxi pulled up in front of the strip club Jaco opened the passenger door and fell out onto the pavement at the foot of a security guard. Then he just lay there for a bit. I saw the taxi driver look down at him with complete contempt. I paid our bill. Fortunately Jaco was known to the club as the guard simply lifted him up and dusted him down and led him in by the arm. I followed behind. I heard someone wolf-whistle at me. They think I'm the main attraction. I thought to myself. I

remember the club was so cold. The air conditioning.
This is a strip club in Siberia. I said to myself. Most of the
girls were wearing cheap swimwear and heels. Purple
bikinis and leopard-print bodices. They were playing
heavy metal music. A woman brought us over a bottle of
awful wine. Do you want a dance. The waitress asked us.
Well. Jaco said. And he looked at me from under his
black greasy fringe that had flopped down over his
forehead. Do you. Sure. I shrugged. I was trying to look
blasé. I could take a dance. Who do you want honeybun.
The waitress asked me. There was a girl with long blonde
curly hair and a little piglet nose that looked like it had
been permanently pressed up against glass when she was
a kid. She was dancing onstage and the DJ was making
affectionate jokes about her. The waitress waved her over
and Jaco handed her a wad of money and just pointed to
me. At first she seemed perturbed. Maybe she had never
been with a woman before. I hadn't. Oh my. Then she
instructed me. Push your chair back against the wall little
one. She said. That gave me a shock. That was my father
speaking. She kneeled up on the chair so that I could
stroke her soft skin. Her beautiful soft skin. And so that I
could smell her too. She smelled like a glamorous baby.
She unhooked her top and her breasts fell out in front of
me. Bite them. She instructed me. I put my teeth on her
huge nipples and pressed down. But it wasn't hard
enough. Bite me. She instructed me again. Really bite me.
Go on. I was afraid to hurt her. But then I thought maybe
they are fake. I didn't know the difference between fake
and real breasts at that point. The only breasts I had to go

on were my own. So I had no comparison. But I thought
maybe if they were fake then they had no feeling left in
them. So it was okay to bite them. I bit them hard and I
thought I might taste blood. But no. She groaned a little
at that and her long hair fell down over my face. Then she
pulled her thong to one side. Put your finger in my
asshole. She said. Can you believe it. Give me your finger
little one. She said. Go on. Then she said please. Please.
Little one. She said. Put your finger up my asshole. I did
what I was told. And it wasn't even clean. I felt a mess
back there. At first I thought I had been tricked. That she
was out to humiliate me by sending me home with a dirty
finger. But really. She was in rapture. I couldn't believe
what you could do to a woman with just your hands. She
slid up and down on my finger with a soft squelching
noise that made me feel like being born all over again.
Soon I got more confident and I pulled her cheeks apart
and put two fingers up there. One finger from each hand.
Then she started bucking. And then she had an orgasm.
Bite me bite me. She said. Give me your fingers little one.
I didn't know you could have an orgasm in your butt at
that point. It was amazing. I felt so proud. That I had put
on such a performance. I felt proud for Jaco to see me.
But when the girl got off me. And started adjusting
herself. When the girl got off me I realised he was
nowhere to be seen. He had paid for my dance and
hadn't even hung around to watch me. I was crushed.
Finally I caught sight of him at the other side of the club.
He was staggering around drunk propositioning other
women. It was pathetic. I loathed him then. The girl

kissed me. And thanked me. And then walked off like nothing had happened. I dared to sniff my own finger. Oh wow. But I decided to keep it to myself. This is my own trophy. I said to myself. Not for pathetic males like Jaco. That's how I felt right then. They switched the lights on in the club and it was home-time. But Jaco was still staggering around propositioning women. They were repulsed by him. So was I.

Let's go. I said to him. And I grabbed him. He was going to be sick and so I had to wait in the reception while he threw his guts up in the toilet. All the time customers kept coming out and saying thank you to me. Thank you. Like I was the star attraction. Then when we got a taxi. When we got a taxi he insisted that we go back to his. My father will be back soon. I warned him. He'll kill me if I'm not there. But he insisted. There's something I want to show you. He said.

When we got back to his place in St. Peters in a street named after a revolutionary hero he pushed me down on the stairs. Then he tried to make love to me. It was pathetic. He was completely incapable and soon he rolled off me and just groaned. Forget it. He said. He was talking to himself then. Wait. He said. There's something I want to show you. Come with me. He said. Then he led me down into his garage. Where an old 1970s motorcycle was parked. It was painted yellow. I don't care about motorbikes. I told him. That's not what I want to show you. He said. And he put his hand inside a rusty metal toolbox and drew out a knife. The blade must have been eight inches long. Look at that. He said. I told you already that Russians love their knives. I'm not playing that game. I told him right away. And then I remembered when I had seen a vision in his mind of me being tied to a chair in my sexy underwear. Oh no. I thought. But really he was a sap when he was drunk. He didn't seem aggressive at all. I felt safe. But that's not what I meant to show you. He said. Then he pulled out something else. Something that was wrapped inside tarpaulin. It was a handgun. Wait a minute. I said. Where did you get that. I found it. He said. I found it in the mud of a river. We were in a heatwave in St. Peters in those days. The rivers had all dried up. Someone must have thrown it in the river. He said. Maybe it was a murder weapon. In that case don't get your fingerprints on it. I said. But he said it was too late. And besides the original prints had probably worn off in the water. Is it loaded. I asked him. I don't know. He said. Why don't you try it. Then he stared at me with his hypnotic eyes. Did I mention he had hypnotic eyes. It doesn't matter because this is where it becomes relevant. Can't you just open the barrel or something and check. I said. I don't think you should do that. He said. I think you should just try it. Don't check it out. He said. I think you should just go ahead and fire it. I took the gun off him. I put it up to my head. Then I asked him to get his camera. I took control of the situation. Get your camera. I said. He looked at me in amazement. Now. I said. And he went scurrying back upstairs. By this point I think he was sober again. In the meantime I examined the gun. It was caked in dry mud. Maybe he was telling the truth. But I didn't open the barrel to see if it was loaded. Besides I had no idea how. Does that camera have a timer on it. I asked him when he came back. In that case set it up on the seat of the motorcycle. Then bring me that knife too. I told him to put the knife up to his throat. Don't even think about it. I said. Just do it. Stand next to me. I told him. And smile for the camera. I thought about the changing forest. Then I put the gun to my head. I thought about a beach in the dark. Then I waited for the camera to flash. I remembered where my finger had been earlier. Then I pulled the trigger.

SYNCHRONICITY IN XSTABETH
by Dana Scallon (Dx(e))

That things happen together and then somehow begin
to relate to one another, somehow draw connections
with one another, invisible connections, in a way, I would
say, connections that at first you are not aware of at all,
like two separate things that just so happen to be going
on at the same time but maybe more than going on,
maybe two separate things (or more in big events, in
major synchronicities) that somehow seem to interact with
each other, though not deliberately, not obviously causally,
though intersect is maybe a better word, not a better
word for synchronicity, synchronicity is the best word to
describe synchronicity and that in itself could be seen as
the ultimate in synchronicity, that a sound or word or set
of letters has come to mean that there is a perfect moment
of synchronicity going on and of course it was coined by
the psychoanalyst and magician (some would say,
especially those who are familiar with *The Red Book*) Carl
Gustav Jung and since then it has become a magic word,
but not like abracadabra, which is a word that precedes a
magical act, whereas synchronicity is a word that bestows
on a certain moment in time the feeling or the observation
or more properly the realisation that moments in time are

made up of lots of mutual or parallel or wildly vectored streams that come together, that intersect, as I said, though intersecting is not synchronicity unless the intersections, in a way, bring information, visual spectacle, ideas or even mathematics or cause and effect together in a way that expands the possibilities of the moment, at least in how the brain organises or predicts or puts the past and the future together, in other words the way the brain conceptualises the movement of various time streams through one moment and out again, the meaning that that intersection has is synchronicity, but in a way it is the word synchronicity, the various streams that meet in that sound, those letters, that concept (and a concept itself is a meeting or intersecting or way of understanding the coming together of certain ideas at one focused point), in other words it is synchronicity that brings synchronicity to bear on synchronicity. But what about coincidence? Well, I would say that coincidence is the opposite of synchronicity. Coincidence is something that makes life mean less. It puts it down. It says "just." "Just" a coincidence. That's why scientists love it. Science (except of course for our great prophets Bruno, Kepler, Newton, Einstein, Sagan, Bohr and their disciples, what a coincidence) is all about "justs" and "onlys." We are "just" a collection of atoms and cells and complex physical processes. God doesn't exist, it was "only" a big bang that started it all. So, when something happens, and you say, well, it was only a coincidence, you have made the decision not to speak the magic word. You have, in effect, said to yourself, I will choose the lesser interpretation, I will choose to remove meaning from the situation, I refuse to anoint these happenings with the magic word of synchronicity. Synchronicity can't happen to me, that's what you're saying, and I'm aware that I am drifting from my point but that's because I took LSD last night because I was feeling bold. I was feeling so bold that I decided to celebrate my newfound boldness by taking some LSD and listening to some music, in this case Bach's *Actus tragicus*, which is funeral music and which at the start has the most remarkable dissonances, blurry notes that almost seem to turn in on themselves like the big bang in music or is that just a coincidence, but like a quiet bang, and what's that saying, the universe begins not with a bang but with a whimper, but I listened to Bach on LSD and I spoke the word synchronicity, as you suggested, I spoke the word and then now, today, here I am, still coming down from LSD, still tripping, as they say, and isn't it true, I believe it is, isn't it true that the founder of Alcoholics Anonymous, I have no idea of his name, it's something that just came to me right now, a moment of synchronicity, I have called it, but didn't he recommend the use of LSD as a way of combatting addiction early on, didn't he think that LSD could be put to good positive psychiatric effect? On LSD, I pronounce that my presence here, in St. Andrews, meeting you, is in fact synchronicity itself, synchronicity across time and space, synchronicity which unites myself with all of this perfect moment, and synchronicity does not simply promise meaningful fun, I realise that, it also contains meaningful sorrow too, but again sorrow that has meaning is not "just" sorrow, sorrow whose end is not simply sorrow but which brings meaning in its wake, well, that too is magic and I pronounce it so: s-y-n-c-h-r-o-n-i-c-i-t-y, I pronounce it so, feeling sad and feeling happy, happy that the next phase of my life can begin, right now, up ahead, finally, but feeling sorrow too, sorrow that this last phase of my life is coming to an end, but I pronounce that synchronicity too, with gratitude, I pronounce it, and I feel blessed and thankful to be caught up in so much meaning.

By the time my father got home. By the time my father got home in the early hours I had been sick all over my bed twice. At first he was annoyed and he took the covers and threw them out of the window. Then he saw the bruising on my head and the burn marks. I told him I had fallen down the stairs. But your head is burnt little one. He said. Friction. I said. It was the only word I could come up with. Then my father started crying. I'm so selfish. He said. I left you at home and you could have died. Meanwhile I'm out chasing my dreams. Even though I was nauseous and dizzy that still hit home. His dreams were just an excuse for a musician more famouser than himself to have sex with his daughter. His dreams were just an excuse for his daughter to take photographs of her own self-murder. His dreams were just a chilly strip club in Siberia. Father. I asked him. How was your night. Although really my eyes were rolling in my head. And I can't remember what he told me. It was only when I saw Jaco that I heard the full story.

In the meantime I had become a ghost. Jaco got the photograph developed. The one with me killing myself in it. My head is a cloud of smoke. Who knew a gun could cause so much smoke. Maybe because it was damp. And we are both looking straight at the camera. Staring deep into it with all our might. The famouser musician is drawing the blade across his throat but not really. There was barely a mark. He was only acting. Whereas I had really pulled the trigger. If I hadn't had my trigger finger in some girl's butthole. If I hadn't had my trigger finger in some girl's butthole earlier I might have scored a direct hit and drilled a hole through my own brain. But my finger slipped. And the gun moved. And the bullet skimmed the back of my head. But in the picture I didn't know that. But in the picture I was a dead girl. I recalled my father on the TV programme. The one with the comedy protest singer. I remember how he said we needed new men. New women. People who did things in blood. Then I thought what was the point. Then I thought about the cowboys murdering the Indians in the pass. Then I realised I was in the saddle. I was in the saddle more than any of them. I realised that the night my father came home in the early hours and threw my blankets out of the window. Even though I was nauseous and I was the one with the sore head I sat back down on my bare bed and stroked his head softly while he wept. I should have been here. He kept saying. It's okay. Little one. I said. I took the words right out of his mouth. It was time. It's okay little one. I said. Everything's okay. Everything's all right. I knew he was crying for lots of things. Some things that I knew about. Some things that I never would. Some things to do with my mother. Some

things to do with the hopelessness of his career. I knew
really it was nothing to do with me. And that was fine.
After that if I needed anyone to talk to I talked to the
photograph. I talked to myself one second before my
death. That's called being enlightened. And it's easy.
When you have seen yourself dead then everything feels
like saying goodbye forever. But then you realise you are
always looking at everything like death is just up ahead. I
would stare at my father as he smoked a pipe and listened
to Leonard Cohen. And Nick Drake. That was another
one. I would stare at him in the light of a candle. And
under my breath I would say bye-bye. Bye-bye. He would
tell me that Nick Drake is dead. Nick Drake died. He
would say. Nick Drake is dead. He killed himself while
listening to the "Brandenburg" Concertos by J. S. Bach.
He was listening to it on LP. On an old stereo. So that it
kept repeating the final bar. That's what he said. He
would say to me *the final bar*. Again and again. And then
he would look at me significantly. I'm hearing the final
bar right now. I would think. And I would look at my
father. My father bent over the old stereo. Nick Drake
had no ego. My father said. Then he shook his head.
Leonard Cohen went into a Zen monastery. He said. That
was because of girls. He said. He was getting too many
girls. Can Zen cure you of women. Not cure you. He said.
But everybody needs a break. Nick Drake said fame was
like a fruit tree. He said. Who needs it. That made no
sense to me. Surely everyone could use a fruit tree. Free
fruit. It's not exactly hard cash. But still.

* * *

There was always dust in our old house. Dust in the air.
You could see it tinkling in the candlelight. That's what
dust does. It tinkles in the light. Normally a shaft of
sunlight. But we didn't see much of those. My father and
I. My father liked to keep the curtains closed. Plus. He
preferred to use candles. Plus. He abhorred central
heating. Plus. He never painted over the damp spots on
the walls. He just let them hang there. It occurred to me
that everything was changing. Everything was breaking
free. Even the tinkling dust. I got up from the armchair
next to the fire. I walked deliberately next door. I chose
to end that scene right then and there. By the time I came
back it was gone forever. Even though my father was still
there. And even though he was still bent over the stereo.
And even though the dust was still spinning slowly in the
air. Still spinning slowly and tinkling. I knew. I knew I
had limited time left with my father. In the slow spinning
and tinkling I knew that time was running out. Still I
knew. It would be easier for me to love him when he was
dead. When he was helpless and dead like a little child.
But what about this precious moment passing in the light
and the dust. To give up to this moment as it is passing.
Can you. I thought I would try my best while he was
alive. The best way I could think to do this was to keep
saying goodbye to him. Under my breath no matter what.
Goodbye. Beautiful moment. Dear father. Goodbye.
Light tinkling. Me. Echoing. Goodbye. Goodbye. But
then I started saying it to rooms and to certain streets and

to whole cities even. And mixing them up. Goodbye City of White Nights. Goodbye old chess piece. Goodbye old shoes laid out to dry. Goodbye peeling wallpaper. Goodbye Church of the Vladimir Icon of the Mother of God. Goodbye strange ornament. Goodbye sad old pigeon-stained monument to Mikhail Lermontov. Goodbye bedroom of my childhood. Goodbye far-off galaxies. Up above. Goodbye rotten fruit bowl. Goodbye Sennaya Ploshchad. Goodbye little warm stove in the living room. Goodbye little smoke rising up. Goodbye tattered old paperback. Goodbye little moon. Up above. Goodbye Bol'shaya Morskaya Ulitsa. Goodbye depressing painting on the wall. Goodbye old penknife. Faded postcard of Marc Chagall. Farewell! Faded postcard of Marina Tsvetayeva curled up with the damp and the cold and with the little spores on it. Goodbye! Faded postcard of Gloria Swanson. I'll be off now! Farewell torn tea towel. Farewell stained teapot. And little box of matches. See you! Golden icon of Xenia. And to friends. Goodbye Marja. Goodbye dear friends. Faithful companions. Farewell! And to the dust itself too. Goodbye old dust. Tinkling. Play me a song about saying goodbye. I asked my father. I know just the one. He said. Then he played me "Hey That's No Way to Say Goodbye." By Leonard Cohen. What is the correct way to say goodbye. I asked him. That's a good question. I'm not sure Leonard Cohen answers it. He said. That's his genius. You would think genius had a few answers to things. I thought. But I held my tongue. I think you say goodbye with gratitude. Do you say it softly. I asked him. Oh yes. He said. The softer the better. My dad was a genius with the answers. That's what I told myself. As I softly told him goodbye. Are things softly said the better. I asked him. Think about it. He said. Would you rather be whispered to. OR SHOUTED AT. A whisper is closer to a last breath. I thought. That is why we are able to love it more. But did Leonard Cohen have to go into a Zen monastery because girls were whispering sweet nothings in his ear. I asked him. He wanted the whispers to last forever. My father said. The nothings. But that's demanding the impossible. Do you miss the whispers. I asked him. The nothings. It was the closest we had come to talking about my mother. Nick Drake has a voice like a constant whisper. He said. And he played a song called "Hazey Jane." That was an up-tempo whisper. It's like he is singing really close to your ear. Besides. He said. I get the whispers. I get them when I play my music. The nothings. He said. I get them when I play my music. And everyone is hushed. And they have to whisper between themselves. If they want to talk. You can hear their breath beneath the guitar strings. Whispering. It's a great feeling. He said. If Nick Drake had no ego why did he kill himself. I asked him. I mean. I said. What was there to kill. His genius turned on itself. He said. And he nodded. As if he understood it all too well. Was he disappointed that he wasn't more successful. I asked him. That too. He said. And he nodded. But fame is just a fruit tree. I told him. He nodded. Maybe that's all he was asking. He said. Then he asked me if I still said my prayers at night. Do you kneel down next to your bed and say your prayers. He asked me. I wasn't sure what the correct answer was. I wondered what Leonard Cohen and Nick Drake thought of prayers. Do Zen people pray. Then I said. I whisper them under my breath. Like I'm talking into the ear of God. That's good. He said. That's fine. What I didn't tell him was that really I had started praying all the time. Every minute under my breath. And that my prayer was saying goodbye to everything.

What did Leonard Cohen die of. I asked him. Leonard Cohen isn't dead. He told me. That didn't make sense according to his records. In that case how did he live. I asked him. He had a song called "Hallelujah" for example. My father said. I think that helped. Would you like me to sing it for you. He asked me. I said yes. Even though I hated my father's singing voice then and felt embarrassed for him. I closed my eyes and kept saying bye-bye bye-bye bye-bye under my breath. Like a mantra till he stopped. To try to get me to like it. Then I smiled awkwardly. I couldn't even make it natural. I was furious with myself. Even though I had a nauseous feeling in my stomach. And my flesh crawled. Is hallelujah the correct way to say goodbye. I wondered. Then I asked it out loud. It's a hallelujah like a last gasp. My father said. Tell me how mum died. I asked him. We had never talked about it really. Because I was too young. He picked up the guitar and strummed it. While he spoke like he was introducing a song. She was on her honeymoon. He said. Then he played a few chords. She was on holiday with her new partner. He said. This was in Bulgaria. He said. This was in the summer. He said. He played a little run on the strings. He began naming the chords as he played. E minor. He said. With her treacherous true love. He said. If this was a song. I thought to myself. If this was a song it would be called "The Treacherous True Love." But then I thought. Why isn't it a song. Is the only reason it's not a song because my father is singing it. Later on I made a list of things that happened after my father died. Things that he would never experience. And even that reads like a song. But somehow when he was alive it was a different story. B. He said. A minor. I'm making these chords up by the way. I can't get his song exactly right. My mum used to sing me a song when I was little. She would sing Aneliya is a lovely girl. She's a lovely baby. E minor. He said. They had gone for a walk on the beach. He sang. All the stars were out. She took her shoes off to feel the sand on her feet. It was the first time she had seen the sea. C. He said. I had never brought her to the ocean. He sang. Never took her to the sea. The sea air and the waves. He sang. Her arms so delicate and small. He sang. Her tiny waist. Her handbag all filled up with treasure. He sang. A minor. And she took off her dress in the rocks and the sand. She untied her loose dress and dived in. She was into the water up to her waist. And she went under and came up again. E minor. Three times she dived. Three times she rose. Three times she went down into the sea. Now she is laughing and looking back up. Now she is nowhere to be seen. I heard they had been drinking earlier that night. C. I heard that there had been a scene. But now the waters are as still as can be. A minor. Now your mother is drowned in the sea. E minor. Now your

mother is drowned in the sea. Little one. Now your
mother is drowned in the sea. How do you know what
happened that night. C. From the true love that won her
hand. How did he win it. Fair and square. He was a
better man than me. A minor. Was she swept beneath the
waves do you think. Or did she dive on her own as if free.
Or did he press a foot down upon her pretty head. So
that she would drown in the sea. We'll never know. My
little one. Not in this life. I'm afraid. But I think of your
mother still tossed in the waves. And not under the
ground asleep. Not under the ground asleep. I said. Do
you think she still moves on the waves. C. I think she still
moves and she'll never be still. She'll never be held in her
grave. A minor. And that's how it is. And how it should
be. That a woman so fair should be free. E minor. Should
be free to be tossed in the dark of the sea. Just as the
world turns. A minor. Endlessly.

Anomic Aphasia in Xstabeth
by Denise Kaufman (SR\SIF)

A nomic aphasia is the feeling that a word is on the tip of your tongue. It is a feeling where a word becomes a sensation, an entity, a ghostly presence whose shape and form you are aware of and yet whose word you are unable to speak. God had much the same problem with the creation of the world, which is why it happened at a specific date and has not been around forever, which every scientist will tell you so.

Anomic aphasia, then, can be seen, equally, to be a feeling that the world is on the tip of your tongue. In the beginning, the prophets write, was the word. But why wasn't it spoken earlier? The big bang, in this scenario, represents the explosive retrieval of the word, the word that was on the tip of God's tongue, and considering that no word up until that point had been spoken, we can well believe that the first word was in fact a saying of the ability to form words, in other words the discovery of the tongue and more particularly, its tiny tip, upon which uncounted angels no doubt danced in its aftermath.

Which is to say that God had forgotten his ability to speak. It was on the tip of his tongue all along. But the tip of his tongue remained to be spoken. The tip in turn would speak the mouth, would sound its limits, which would then speak the throat, and the lungs, which coupled articulation to volume, to great booming basso volume and vibrato, even, befitting a/the God.

This process of the formation of the House of God can be tracked throughout Genesis.

Handy hint: the Hebrew letter for mouth is Pey/Fey (פ) whose number is eighty and which also can be taken to stand for word, expression, vocalisation and breath.

Handy hint: God remembered the world when he spoke it.

But what of the teeth? Speech makes much ado of the teeth, which any linguist worth their "salt" (handy hint) will tell you so. There are thirty-two teeth in the mouth of a human.

Handy hint: the Kabbalistic tree of life, which itself is derived from the repeated appearance of god-angels in Genesis, has thirty-two paths of wisdom.

Handy hint: the term anomic aphasia relies for its pronunciation on four alephs whose number is one. Four.

Extra handy hint: the Hebrew letter for the House of God is Beth (ב) whose number is two.

Next comes our turn to speak.

But will we (final handy hint) "remember"?

Did you hear about the satellite. The one they sent into space. Seduced out of the world. Only to look back down on it. That was me. For a few months at least. I was like that. Unmanned probes. They call them. An empty echo. Always saying goodbye. Do you know things have seasons. Not just forests. Everything has seasons. I told that to Jaco. Everything has its season. I said. Who's that. He said. Epicurus. I actually got it from Bob Dylan. You and I. I said. You and I will have our season. What season is that. He said. Oh. It's spring. I said. I knew he wanted me to say it was autumn. Or something more poetic. The universe is infinite and eternal. I said. But still it likes to be done with things and get them over with all the same. He was telling me about my father's performance on the night I died.

There had been about twenty people in the audience. Which I didn't think was too bad. Jaco heard the story from the club promoter who had done him the favour in the first place. He said that my father turned up and made a big fuss about emptying the club. Emptying the club so he could soundcheck in privacy. Then he asked to

be shown to the green room. There was no green room.
But they bought him a vodka and let him sit at the bar.
Then they broke the news that there was a support act.
Didn't Jaco tell you. He fumed. No support. We need it
for the door. The promoter said. To get people in. My
name gets people in. My father supposedly said. Then the
guy turned up. A young guy with messy hair and an
acoustic guitar. He had a set of keys connected to the belt
of his jeans by a chain. No key janglers. My father kept
saying. Until it got awkward and the guy had to take his
keys off and put them in his pocket. This guy was playing
all original material. This is like Donovan never
happened. My father is supposed to have said. When my
father got onstage he did a Bert Jansch thing. Which I
didn't know what that meant. But apparently it means a
complicated piece that people in folk clubs challenge each
other with. The young guy was trying to be friendly. Or so
they say. That shreds. He said. Or something young like
that. Shreds. My father is supposed to have said. Shreds. I
shred my skin every time I pick up a guitar sunshine. I
don't think he would have used the word sunshine. But
then Jaco said it was probably a Donovan in-joke. I shred
my skin. He is supposed to have said. And then I drive a
guitar string straight into a vein. And then I'm cooking. I
don't think he would have said that either. But that's how
it was reported. The Donovan guy played his set. It was
good. My father was drunk. There was a drum kit
onstage. As my father was getting ready to go on someone
came up to him. Who knows what he looked like. He's
lost now. But he was breathing hard and had his hair in

his face. It was likely he was on drugs. If you suck. He
said. If you suck I'll get up onstage and join you on
drums. He said. To my father. My father was intimidated.
For a moment. Who says that kind of thing. But then he
just went on with tuning his guitar. Then he makes a
decision. Or perhaps he had made it already. Perhaps it
was the Donovan guy being so good. Perhaps it was the
lack of respect from the drummer. Perhaps it was because
there were only twenty people in the room. But he
decides to make up a whole set of songs on the spot. Now
original songs were not my father's hot spot. He was an
imitator. A tribute act. I have to be honest. This was a
radical step. This was more like a tightrope walk at the
circus. He comes onstage and he sits down on a stool.
The room goes quiet. There's some of that quiet
whispering that we talked about. Nothings. Then he sings
these two lines. It's so cold. He sings. In the summertime.
That's all. Again. And again. In this pained voice. In this
pained voice like it's beamed in from another planet.
Then more lines. Mountains yes mountains. He sings.
Then he plays a one-string solo by de-tuning the bottom
E string on his guitar. Someone said it was like Kundalini.
A new-age person. Obviously. Which is when a serpent
crawls up your spine. There were more soft whispers in
the audience. Then the drum guy gets up from the
audience and sits behind the kit. There's no way of
knowing if my father saw him get up or not. All the time
he was singing and playing the guitar with his eyes closed.
But of course he hears him when he comes in. And the
drummer plays this march. This crazy off-tempo march.

And it's like a legion of ghosts marching right through the music. Right through the mountains. In the cold of the summer. Then he sang some more. My father. Is it not for kings. He sang. My father. Is it not for kings. This summer. Who knows where he was coming from by this point. And the drummer starts rubbing his hand over the skin of the drum. Like he was stroking the pale yellow skin of a dying man. So gently. Whispering. It was like classical portraiture. Someone said. They play on. My father teases slow single notes from the guitar. It's like it is expiring. There's a back and forth between the soft drums and the notes like tiny heartbeats. Then the drummer gets up. He gets up and crosses the stage. Then he steps onto the floor. Then he walks across the room and up the stairs. Then he walks straight out of the club and into the street. And is never seen again. My father sat still on the stage for some time. There was awkward applause. No one knew what to think. Then he came home and threw my sick covers out of the window. Then he cried in my lap and regretted everything.

MEMORY IN XSTABETH
by Frances McKee (Dx(e))

If you were able to witness a memory coming into existence—and the technology is here and available right now according to all accounts—then it would appear like a star being born in a far-off galaxy. Science had a hunch—and then proved it—that memories are synaptic transmissions stored in things called neurons. Everything we do is stored in neurons or is being shot straight to the heart of a neuron as soon as it takes place, though with varying degrees of power and/or retrievability (is that even a word?) according to the significance of the event. This is where we come to the first of many—some might say infinite—impasses. Why do some memories affect us so? Why do they stay with us for life while others are shrugged off as if even the neurons themselves were unconvinced of their import or the point of going to all that infinitesimally small effort to store them in the first place? Is significance built up over time? For instance, do neurons tend towards specific focuses in terms of storage according to the weight of impact of the events, like suns exploding into life as opposed to the arrival of mild weather systems? Where does significance come from? Neurons would seem to be neutral; we presumed that when we named them. But all memory is not stored equally. But at first, you would think, it must be. Who or what decides on the significance of early childhood experience? Neurons, you would think, store everything that happens objectively and without weight or bias. Whereas babies—early on, at least—would appear to do the same. At first there is no discriminatory factor involved. Things happen and they are stored. Now, you could say, well, the brain is only forming then, it is still growing. Okay, then why do developmental psychologists and biologists and genetic scientists and a veritable roll call of who's who across the professions all insist that early experiences tend to dominate, to fix character, to establish neuroses, to effectively set shape to the future? But the question still remains, why are early childhood memories not exhaustive compared to fickle adult memories when things like beliefs, wants, desires, perceived values, personality traits and the whole identity thing are more likely to get in the way and privilege the storage of certain experiences over others?

But memory retention is actually a very precarious business, a virtual tightrope walk across an abyss of forgetting, if you will excuse the imposition of poetry, but I'm afraid that may become unavoidable if we are to fully get to grips with the enormity of our subject. Memories are formed by what we (science) have come to term "messenger RNA" or even better "mRNA." These are messengers that encode protein just like writing in a journal or better still carving hieroglyphics into a block of (soft) stone, if you can encode that in your protein, ha ha. That was a scientific joke by the way. We may have more use of them too, as we continue down this path.

Proteins, in turn, shape and restructure cells in the neurons. So, let's say you see a handsome young man on the beach in St. Andrews in 1993, let's say. The sight of the man in his shorts with the water lapping around his calves and the dark hair on his chest and the dark eyes too, the muscular arms, standing there in the water without a care in the world, his hair like a Fifties rock star, this stimulates the hippocampus, which is the region of the brain that deals with making memories. Now, you will remember this man to this day. It is so vivid, it's almost like he is alive in here. What has happened is that the force of this vision, the bare fact of this man, standing there in the waves, standing there with what appears to be a makeshift raft in his hand, a makeshift raft against all that ocean, well, it's enough to encode protein. And that is not a euphemism. Ha ha, that is another scientific joke just as I predicted would be irresistible earlier. Then we have a glorious moment of synthesis across an infinitely small expanse, although in reality the expanse is as breathtaking, and as impossible, as the spans between the stars themselves. I told you poetry would come in handy too.

So the protein-encoding mRNA goes to work on the nucleus of the neuron, which we can compare to a great

artist so in love with the world and all he sees and who is
haunted by a particular image, a single image that he
spends his entire career, gives his life and his health to
rendering, perfectly, just once. Only this happens in a
time and space that is basically inaccessible to human
beings. We simply see the result. And I use the word
"see" although really memory is something that makes use
of all the senses while refusing any one of them
completely. So as we track the newly transformed
molecules, the newly sculpted proteins, and follow them
all the way to the dendrites, where communication
between neurons takes place, we feel as if the very same
sun is beating down on us from that day in 1993, we see
the man's dark shorts, the white string-pull on their waist,
we smell the seaweed and feel the sand and broken shells
under our feet and we smell the man too; he smells of
old-fashioned aftershave and of holidays, oddly enough,
which might just be the suntan lotion speaking, the
suntan lotion, itself, speaking to proteins and neurons and
in blinding flashes in the brain, and we have an amazing
feeling, as if everything that ever was is speaking and will
never stop, just like stars won't stop appearing even if
they were all to fall from the sky overnight.

That was when I told Jaco about seasons and satellites.
It's my father's season. I told him. No one saw it
coming. Except maybe he did. Then his season became a
summer. But a secret summer. One that you keep to
yourself. It turns out that one of the people who worked
at the bar there was a music fanatic. That he had an old
reel-to-reel recorder set up in the room. That something
had struck him about my father's performance. That he
had recorded it. Almost from the start but not quite. But
most of it was there. He was so perplexed by the music
that he wanted to put it out. But then he said the music
was making demands of him. That's exactly what he said.
Like it was a prison warden in a gulag. Or a member of
the secret police. It demanded anonymity. He said he was
listening to the music. He said he had no option. That the
music demanded to be released. But under a veil. Was
what he said. Then it told him its name. It said its name
was Xstabeth. That's what it said. Xstabeth.

After all it isn't unusual for music to speak to people. It
spoke to my father all the time. It isn't unusual for music
to make demands on people. But I was like that. What.

But it is unusual for it to give you its name. Plus. In the circumstances to give you a name like that. Like what. Like a king. I thought. Or like a princess. Like a demon princess. But maybe that's just the lyrics getting to me. But it was the lyrics that spoke it. Not just the lyrics. The music too. The drummer too. The secret drummer. He was spoken. You could say. Not just the drummer. The night was spoken. Not just the night. The date with the famouser musician. That was spoken too. Don't you see. And the gunshot. The gunshot that went off in my head. And me dying and coming back to life. That was spoken too. And now it all had a name. And then it had a life of its own. That's the next thing. Months go past. We know nothing of all this. All this about the music speaking in secret at this point. Maybe deviously. Maybe it was speaking in a devious tone. I can accept that. But the point was it had to go behind our backs. It had to play the cards it was dealt. So it wasn't really devious. It was just being practical in a practical way. Like when a snake crawls up into a thick tree. It's just being practical. Because of the cool shade. And the hot earth. But when it leaps down on you and constricts you. When it pulls you up into the tree. Wrapped all around you. You think that's devious. You think snake eyes you had a plan. An improvisation might be more true. Old snake eyes. So you give it a break. Even though the whole thing seems creepy and malevolent. But really snake eyes are empty. It's just doing its thing. As its mouth swallows your head. Oh dear. So Xstabeth was just doing her thing. I'm going to call her her. But I could just as easily call her him. I think.

Not it. Though a snake is it. Though not really. Alive. Is what I'm trying to say. Alive and sexy. You can't deny that of a snake. Even if it causes you to leap out of your skin.

So a record came out but we never found out. And a weird coincidence happened. Another improvisation. I became pregnant by the famouser musician. But no longer the notoriouser musician. But wait for that. First off. I find out that I am up the duff. As they say. How delightful. That I am preggers. As they say. It was like a rebound. From my death. Double the life in return. We finally made love. Jaco and I. We made love in the back of his Viva every chance we got. It was like being in a drive-in movie. All the panting and the steam and the hands against the windows. The crazy positions. I can vouch for that. I liked sex. But then I liked holding a gun up against my head. So it was no surprise. I got an STD too. At first. I mean. I had a discharge. I know you have other partners. I told him. Lucky for you. He said. That was all. I accepted it. I wasn't planning on getting married. Until I got pregnant. Then I said to myself. I can't go on saying bye-bye anymore. I was just being practical. I was just playing my own hand. We need two for this baby. I said to myself. But then I thought of my father. Things were getting complicated. This could push him over the edge. Then the record came out and changed everything.

How we found out about it is my father would go to this folk bar. It was a bar run by a guy who suffered from facial elephantiasis. You know the Elephant Man. Yes. Exactly. But he was a cool guy. He made bootleg cassettes. And stocked LPs of stuff you couldn't get in Russia. My father would go there. And the room was tiny. So tiny. Like five stools. And a bar. That was it. He brewed his own beer. And he played records at the same time. Roy Harper. Jackson C. Frank. Bob Desper. Sky Saxon. All the greats. And one night my father is in there alone. Drinking. It's no surprise. And The Snork. That's what he was known as. The bar was called Snork's. The Snork puts on this LP. Says nothing. Just pours another beer and stands there. And then drinks it with half the contents going down his shirt. With his face being like that he could hardly get a drink in his mouth. So the bar was always running at a loss. Really he was making money from selling records and tapes. He had to. So. He stands there. And he says nothing. With this beer all over him. At first my father doesn't react. Then he looks up at The Snork. He looks up in amazement. We would have to say. Or puzzlement. He looks up in puzzlement. Let's say. The Snork looks back at him and nods. Just nods. We can't say if he is smiling. Or if he is serious. Or if his mouth is open in awe. Because his face got in the way. But he's nodding and looking straight at my father. We can see that. Then the singing comes in. It's so cold. In the summertime. What the hell is this. My father explodes. The thing is. And this is what he said later. The thing is he both recognised it as himself while thinking that the voice was coming from someone else entirely. At first. And this is insane. At first he thought it was a cover version. Or even the original of the song. Oh my lord. He said. Had I heard this before and forgot it. Then I played it from a distant memory. Is that what happened. That can happen you know. Like being haunted by a song. But that only lasted a split second. Before he could say any more The Snork kept on nodding. And then he said. I know. In a muffled voice. I know. In a muffled voice. It's fucking incredible. Isn't it. I knew you'd like it. The Snork said. I knew it was right up your street. This is the sound of the underground man. He said. Wait. This is on LP. My dad said. Someone released this. He said. It's hard to believe. The Snork mumbled. But yes. Someone put this out on vinyl. Then he handed my father the sleeve. Then he saw the name Xstabeth. Then he froze like that.

He came back home and he told me. I'm a ghost. I'm a ghost. He said. I thought I was the one that was supposed to be dead. Then I thought I had cast a spell on us. I began to think that after all maybe I was Xstabeth. Maybe I had cast us all into twilight. I began to think that my little baby was a ghost too. A ghost pregnancy. That can happen. I said to Jaco. I'm starting to doubt the reality of you. Solipsism. He said. No. I said. I knew that one. No. I said. I doubt me too. Buddhism. He said. No. I said. It's like touching without touching. Zen Buddhism. He said. No. I said. It's as if there is no volition. Determinism. He said. Like all we are is ghosts. Idealism. He said. I feel so unhappy. Nihilism. I'm tired of your lists. Logophobia. I think I'm a female demon. Goetia.

Then my father made a startling decision. I was like that.
What. He said that we would tell no one. Tell no one little
one. He said. Tell no one. And it was like being buried
alive. The arrival of Xstabeth. Like being sealed in a
secret tomb with my father. Then Jaco heard about it. He
said to me don't tell your father who did it. And of course
the guy who recorded it was telling no one. Under the
instructions of Xstabeth. And the promoter of the club.
He didn't keep up with new music. How would he know.
And the 20 people who were in the club. They were there
to see the Donovan character. What would they know.
And would anyone remember. And then the reviews
started coming in. In the underground journals. Then The
Snork began selling the record by the boxload. Then the
rumours started up. The rumour was that it was a
bluesman who had sold his soul to the devil. At a
crossroads. And then disappeared forever. The rumour
was that it was a suicide note. The rumour was that it was
a mental patient on day release. The rumour was that it
was a famous musician in disguise. The rumour was that
it had been recorded in a cave. At night. And that the
audience had been led there in blindfolds. The rumour
was that it was a religious meeting. A strange sect. The
rumour was that it was a recovering UFO abductee. The
rumour was that it was a séance. The rumour was that it
was a dead man. My father's mood changed. He would
say things like. She's a cult hero. Referring to himself.
Then he would say. This is it. This is what I've always
wanted. For her. He would add. I remembered my
mother. Still alive in the sea. And me too still alive. And

my father too. Somehow still alive. I tried to put it
together like a puzzle. Like who's alive and who's dead.
Then I realised it was already in place. Silly me.

* * *

I moved out of my father's house. He wasn't lonely
anymore. I thought. But first I got my buck teeth fixed.
I had cute buck teeth. I didn't tell you that. That's how
me and Marja became friends. We were the buckies. The
bucky gang. The Bugs Bunnies. I asked my father. Can I
go to the dental hospital. I thought you liked your
buckies. He said. You can't be a Bugs Bunny forever. I
said. Well you can but it looks like neglect. He took me
to the hospital. He waited outside while they examined
me. They brought lots of students over. I was a test case.
It seemed. I was a real Bugs Bunny. They crowded
around. They talked about me like I wasn't there. All the
time I had my mouth wide open. I could feel the air
drying my insides. I could feel the sharp metal on my
teeth. They all leaned in. I thought they were going to
start climbing down my throat. One by one. I thought
they were going to put a small metal ladder in there.
And climb right down. First. They put mirrors in. Like
they were decorating a room. Then. They shone a light
in there. Like they were playing a game at the
fairground. Everyone looked in. They're just looking for
their own face in my mouth. I thought. It was like group
sex. Or how I imagined it. Plus. They all had white
hospital coats on. And the nurses had nylons. I heard

they wore stockings all the time. I heard it was because tights generate static electricity at the gusset when they walk. The gusset. What a word. And it disrupts the machines. I thought everyone is in their underwear beneath their clothes. I know it sounds obvious. But it was the first time I had thought it. There are lots of things you haven't thought which if you did would be remarkable. I imagined everyone posing in their underwear in the mirrors in my mouth. Like in a private changing room. All the mirrors. I'm echoing again. I thought to myself. I'm echoing again. I'm echoing again. Then someone said. Here comes the father. Here he comes. They said. And it was as if everyone hurriedly buttoned up their clothes. And smoothed down their coats. And fixed their hair. My father was in the ward. I saw him striding towards us. Really striding. What a motion. His handsome physique. He had become emboldened. Emboldened by Xstabeth. Excuse me. He said. And took control of the situation. But what the hell is going on here. He said. It was like he had read my mind. Everyone backed off like the ripples from a pebble. This is a special girl. My father said. This isn't a zoo. Really he should have said S&M funfair. But I was touched. I was moved. I lay there in the chair with a tube in my mouth. And my mouth fixed open. And the lonely satellite was back. But she was discovering new planets. And she was relaying the good news. I took the clamp out of my mouth. And the tube too. Then I spun round in my chair for effect. Then I took my father's hand. Then I walked off. Swaying my hips this way and that. You can bet. On my high heels. Like they didn't know what to think.

When I tell you it like that it sounds like a dream. Doesn't it. Like a dream full of symbols. We have been taught that dreams are populated by symbols. Which makes it hard to see dreams as they are. We are always asking what did my father stand for. What did the ladder down my throat mean. Had they come to take my baby. Did I really not want my baby. I imagined it being carried up the ladder from my stomach and out of my throat. Like Moses in a basket. What about the teeth. Don't they always say that teeth mean sex. Or what. But where does it end. If a symbol reveals a symbol. I mean where does it stop. I think it is trying to say there is no solid ground. But in a world of ghosts I had found my solid ground. It was my father. He had become the new man. Like he had predicted. But not exactly. He had believed that the new man would be bloody. Do you remember. He had boasted about that before he became the new man. Or the new woman. But really the new man was dependable and light. He went back to Snork's and he bought a copy of the LP. It's selling like crazy. The Snork told him. This guy is a cult hero. My father would sit in the living room. With the dust tinkling in the candlelight. He would pick up his guitar and try to play along. He couldn't do it. He was relieved. This is singular. He said. This is music that cannot be repeated. This is music that can never be toured. This is music that can never be applauded. I pointed out to him that there was applause on the record.

Muted applause. Awkward applause. Uncomprehending
applause. But still. Applause. What is the sound of one
audience member clapping. I asked him. He laughed. Yes.
He said. Yes. Yes. There is no mechanic in the world for
this music. He said. I really don't know if I understood
him. But I had to let him speak. Did he mean that this
music could never be repaired. Did he mean it could
never be rationalised. Did he mean it was so wounded it
could never be made whole. Or did he mean there was no
system. No culture. No means. Did he mean we were
right back at the end of symbols.

* * *

And with that my father stopped. He stopped making
music. He stopped worrying about art. And his place in
art. He had come through art. I realised. Was what he
said. Or he might have said. I am realised. Or I have
realised. Either way. He had come to the end. The point
of art is to be done with it. He said. With a sigh. Of relief.
Or maybe just a sigh. The point of art is to get you to the
place where you have no need of it. Art is a neurotic
activity. He said. That's why there is so much more of it in
the city. The end of art is at the end of the world. He said.
I thought he might take up gardening or something. But
really he cultivated doing nothing. He just sat there for
hours.

Still he kept up with Xstabeth. What she was up to. He
kept up with the reviews. The way you keep up with your

daughter's exam results. We entered a period of great calm. Which coincided with my pregnancy. Which I still hadn't revealed to my father. I'm old enough to have my own apartment. I said to him. Brashly. Besides. I told him. Besides I got a job in a florist. It's time for me to support myself. He didn't argue. Previously he would never have let me go. But we went looking for flats together. We agreed on one that overlooked a river. This was in the winter and the river was frozen. But rivers freeze in the winter. It was no more than that I tell myself now.

EQUILIBRIUM IN XSTABETH
by Maureen (indecipherable) *(Dx(e))*

* (*indecipherable*) strategy (*indecipherable*) equilibrium for (*missing*)

This model was the concept of (*missing*)

equilibrium. That is, in the case of three (*missing*)

over a uniformly distributed set of entries, (*missing*)

(*missing*) converge in the middle and succeed with a (*missing*)

(*missing*) the parties separating infinitesimally

(*missing*) piece.

(*missing*) one piece is who

(*missing*)d it will be (*missing*)

The sound of the trees at night. When I was pregnant and lived all alone. The sound of the forest at night. An elegant woman fussing over a grave. Then a shuffling of cards. The soft shuffling of a deck of cards. Then the river cracking. The frozen river cracking in the warmth of the stars. Then the bats. Tunnelling. Digging round tunnels through the air. Then my baby. My baby kicking. Backwards. My baby kicking backwards. Heeling. Soft heeling. Then the reflux. Terrible acid reflux. The sight of my father. Asleep on the couch. Curled up asleep with his long hair and his socks. His shoes. His little shoes tucked under the couch. Tiny toes.

My father would stay over. He would take me to the supermarket. Buy me sliced ham and coffee and white bread. And yoghurt. He would insist on yoghurt. And a cucumber. For the sandwich. And he would turn up at odd hours. He would call through the letterbox. Little one. He would say. Little one I brought you a wooden banister from the old house. I brought you a memento. And I would have to sneak Jaco out. Through the window. Through the window in full sight of the whispering forest. And across the frozen river. Which would crack as he went. It was a season of DIY. Of my father building bookcases for me. Bookcases where the shelves ran this way and that. And a desk. A desk that was too high. A desk that was too high so he built a chair on a raised platform so I could reach it. He was resourceful that way. Then he would go back to sitting. Sitting by the window and staring out. Yawning and stretching and staring out contentedly. Content with the way things had worked out. I would say. Content with how his dreams had come true but in an unusual way.

My father was becoming emotional too. Secret tears. He would cry easily. At the sight of a deaf boy pointing at a toy on a high shelf. At the sight of two young lovers moving in across the road. The sight of them carrying boxes with all their possessions in them. The sight of The Snork. Stood on his own behind the bar. Cueing up God knows what lonely racket. Has he entered his dotage. I asked myself. At night he would stay over and he would read to me. *The Lives of the Saints* was a big favourite. St. Camillus was grieving. Athanasius sought refuge. People offered songs to the guardian angels.

We ate out often. My father liked to wine and dine me. Why not. He would say. He had a favourite fish restaurant where they began to get to know him. The usual table. They would say. We made a point of getting dressed up. Tuesday was date night. That's what we called it. The usual dish was lemon sole. Buttery lemon sole in

the French style. With stewed cucumbers. My father had
started reading cookbooks as a hobby. Things were as
peaceful as that. I thought this could go on forever. My
father and me. With love on the side. But my baby was
ticking down inside me. Things would have to change. I
would get teary myself. When I was on my own. And
once I even cursed the baby inside of me. Do you think
they can feel it. Do you think they know.

Then the unthinkable happened. A new Xstabeth record
was released. My father had been drinking at Snork's.
Fighting back secret tears no doubt. The bomb just
dropped. The Snork announced. What do you mean. My
father went to say. But before he could say anything The
Snork handed him an LP. It's Xstabeth. The Snork said.
He's back. Before he could correct him and say *she's* back
The Snork started playing the LP. It was similar to the
first one. But the guitar playing was slicker. This is a fake.
My father insisted. This isn't Xstabeth. Then a voice came
in. Deeper and more affected than his own. It was singing
about rivers. About crossing frozen rivers. And about a
forest. A forest that spoke in a low voice. I'm not buying
this. My father told The Snork. This is mere poetry. He
said. This doesn't have the feel of the first. This is genius.
The Snork maintained. This is the best yet. Then he
scratched his strange face.

It's not even the same singer. My father maintained. The
Snork shrugged. The rumour is that Xstabeth is a group.
He said. Ridiculous. My father said. The music of

Xstabeth is not the kind of music that is made by committee. What do you think this is. Band Aid.

He called on me through the letterbox. Little one. He said. He sat on the edge of the couch that he had bought me. More tears. The muse isn't loyal to just one man. I tried to say. The muse isn't faithful. But she was mine. He said. I was her. That's what he said. The trees stood motionless. The river had begun to melt. I held my breath. The frozen trees and the talking river. I thought. I got it the wrong way round. Then I thought.

I'm mirroringOgnirorrim m'I.

Who knew about the trees and about the river and about the forest. And about Xstabeth too. Jaco knew. Jaco knew for sure. The only other one was my unborn baby. Who was kicking backwards again and again. The only other one who knew hadn't even been born yet. And would it ever be. That's how you feel when a secret baby is inside you.

* * *

For a week it was peaceful. Then my father returned late one night. I've spoken with Xstabeth. He said. I've heard from the source. What did she say. I asked him. As I made him a ham and cucumber sandwich. With the crusts cut off. His favourite. She says I can't reveal that it is me. That would go against it all. That would be a betrayal. She said. I had done the right thing. She said. Up till now.

I asked her about the other Xstabeth. The new recording.
What did she say. I asked him. It was awkward. He said. I
asked her to deny it. To disown it. To make an example of
it. She let me talk. Sure. She let me talk. But she just sort
of listened. Listen to yourself. I think that was the lesson.
Then she said one simple thing. One simple thing before
she went. What was the one simple thing she said. I asked
him. Prove your love for me. He said.

* * *

I invited Jaco around on a Thursday night. Which was the
night my father took his cookery class. Maybe he'll meet
someone and give us all peace. Jaco said. You'll regret
saying that when he's dead. I told him. But Jaco just lit a
cigarette and stared at me as if to say he would burn up
much faster. Then he lifted me up and positioned me on
the stairs. Did I tell you he had a thing for stairs. He said
you got much better positions that way. That there was
more scope for limbs and curves and for vistas. That's
what he called them. Vistas. He would position me on the
stairs in my underwear with the red heart and with my
heels on. Then he would stand above me and beneath me
and to the side. Then he would ask me to push up on one
hand. Or raise my butt in the air. Or turn my head back.
Or move my foot to a different stair. This would go on for
some time. And the stairs were draughty. But I knew I
was driving him crazy. Who is it that is dancing at the
beginning of the world. And the end too. Is it Shiva.

Afterwards I brought up the new Xstabeth. It was you wasn't it. I said. You're in competition. Why can't you admit it. It was you all along. I said. And by that I hinted at darker things. I have done so much for your father. He said. So much that he will never know. So much that he could never thank me for. Did you know my mother. I asked him. Oh I knew her. He said. I knew her. But you're not ready for that now. For some reason I let him say that and I accepted it. Now I don't know why. Maybe it was the baby talking. What will we do about the baby. I asked him. I'll stand by you. He said. I'll stand by you if you want to have it. But he never once said the word we. It's my father I'm worried about. I said. But of course it was me and the baby I was worried about. But I wanted to seem strong. But I was worried about my father too. Would it be the final straw. I felt like I was being batted about like a little ball. Between these two men like a little tennis ball. Jaco was already drunk. I had bought him a bottle of vodka. And he had started in on it. You can't stay the night tonight. I told him. My father is coming early in the morning. To take me to the supermarket. My father my father my father. He said. In a mocking voice. Get over here and suck me off. He said. We had already done it once. But I kneeled down in front of him on the couch and did it anyway. But he went soft in my mouth and passed out like a deflated balloon. I wondered if my mother had done the same. If my mother had kneeled before him and sucked him off until he passed out. It was a terrible thought. Blowing the same balloon. How pointless. Even so I sat next to him on the couch with his

head rolled back. With his trousers around his ankles.
And with a little juice coming from the head of his penis.
And making it stick to his hairy leg. And I stroked his
hair and his forehead while he snored. There is no
mechanic. I said to myself. Things just carry on.
Regardless.

* * *

Jaco was on TV. My father and I watched it at my flat. He
said he believed in the unspeakable visions of the
individual. He said utopia was totalitarian. He said
immorality was a programme of self-liberation. He said
suffering was a gift. Then he moved on to praising God.
But first we watched the golf.

Of course they showed golf in Russia. Everyone was crazy
about it. Because everyone was an armchair athlete. For
Russians the pace was right. Outdoor sports are not our
thing. That's why we like gymnastics and boxing and ice
hockey. But if we have to go out we like to walk on grass.
Slowly. And take our time. And stare at the horizon with a
meaningful look. And put our hand up to our forehead.
Then shake our head and walk on. Walk on with a hunted
look. Trying to read the landscape. Trying to decode
everything. For a Russian everything's symbolic. That's why
we come alive in books. And why we like golf so much.

Then the talk show came on. Jaco was wearing a suit with
large lapels. And a rust-coloured tie. And a stained yellow

shirt. His hair was unwashed. And he hadn't shaved. He looked sexy and out of control. The topic was utopia. The building of a socialist utopia. How close were we. How far had we come. Where were we going. And why. There were other guests too. It was what they call a round-table discussion. There was a science-fiction author. There was a politician. There was an actor. And the moderator was Anatole Brezhnev. Jesus Jaco is drunk. My father said. It's obvious. He was laughing at the science-fiction writer while he spoke. While he spoke about the goal as being out there. While he prophesied utopian colonies in space. Where technology would render work pointless. And everyone equal. Where leisure was a birthright. We can seed our own garden of Eden on the barren surface of the moon. He said. Or something. The universe is ours. Or something. Hand in hand with technology. Or something like that. Jaco spluttered and lit a flagrant cigarette. He called the science-fiction writer a crypto-hippy and a fascist. What. Do you intend to legislate death out of existence. He mocked him. The idea that there is somewhere to go and something to do is a fallacy. A fallacy that humankind has been in thrall to now for centuries. He took a great glug of water and almost choked on it. Then he said. This is it. He said. This is it. And he slammed the water jug down on the table. My father said it was like a Zen master caning a pupil. He still admired Jaco. That much was clear. Wake the fuck up and see where we are right now. Jaco said. There was consternation in the studio. Language please. Brezhnev said. You're drunk. The actor said. You've been drinking.

Jaco sat there and stared at him with his mad red eyes. That's right I've been drinking. He said. Because I'm alive. Because I'm alive I've been drinking to God's health. He said. God is dead. The politician mocked him. We buried God in 1917. But the heart would not believe. Jaco replied. My father nodded at that one. Then the actor piped in. How can you praise immorality and toast God at the same time. God makes everything possible. Jaco said. Thank God. What of the devil. Brezhnev quizzed him. Why wasn't the devil buried in 1917. Jaco said. There is no devil that's why. He continued. There is one God only. Everything is holy. He said. Suffering is holy. Drunkenness is holy. Birth and death are holy. Only we need a new word for death. He said. Birth and birth again. He said. Birth and birth eternal. Isappearing. He said. Then he took a can of beer that he had secreted in his pocket and opened it with a spray. What a performance. My father marvelled. This is a real Russian performance. Anyone care to drink to that. Jaco said. No one moved. Despite your disbelief. Jaco said. God never gave up on any of you. What a guy. He said. And with that he drained his can in one go. Then he crushed it with relish. Then he let out a burp. Then he tossed it over his shoulder and walked off on live television. He's in for it. My father said. What a guy.

TRUE LOVE IN XSTABETH
by David W. Keenan

True love is when you see yourself out there, in the
world, completely, and when you forgive yourself,
also, because it is hardest to forgive the devil, yet artful,
for it was he, among all of God's angels, who was most in
love with the spirit, and who most begrudged gifting it,
entombing it, in the flesh, which is the art of love.

Love is tied up with birth, and death, and is its third. Its
third being part of the trinity required for the game of
love. I love because of gifts, and because I abound. And
because of endings I am in love with beginnings. I
abound by the seashore, and I give myself up to the
waves. I accept angel names as they are given, without
question. I have been haunted and occupied by places,
just as I have haunted them in return. I am jealous of all
that the world will spend on unknown others. I have
pursued youth as I have pursued the most rarefied ideas,
as I have pursued distances; in longing. My experience of
angels is real. While thoughts have bound me. Still, I
write in gratitude. For all of the impossible detail.
Meeting you. For all of the endless nuance. Of rivers, and
barren trees, of golf, and pale ale, and lingerie. And for

the way in, and out. You who have answered all of my questions as endings without questions is, I name you, beginnings. It is you I have sung after; after you I have implored. You; I'm an idiot. But to bear to let go is only to be in your arms.

I'm taking up art again. My father announced. This was one evening. I thought you had come out the other side of art. I said. I thought you had finished with it. I thought that was the point. The point of art. But you have to really be done with it. My father said. You have to wash your hands of it completely. You have to be able to walk away and not look back. No loose ends. He said. Won't there always be loose ends. I said. Won't it never be tied up. You can say what you want to say and damn the rest. My father said. He was thinking of Jaco. I knew it. He was thinking of Jaco walking off the TV set and disappearing. Because that is exactly what he had done. No one had heard from him since. He had walked off the set and out into the snow and disappeared down a snowy side street in St. Peters never to be seen again. It was exactly like the secret drummer. But this time more personal. Of course there were rumours. That he had slipped and fallen into the frozen river in his drunken state. That happened all the time. Maybe he had tried to come to me. I thought. Maybe he had tried to come to me and had tried to cross the frozen river. Maybe he had tried to cross the frozen river so that he could signal beneath my window. So that he could signal to see if the coast was clear. Maybe even now he was there beneath the water behind my apartment. Like a saint in a glass coffin. Or maybe he had been kidnapped and done in by the secret service. Maybe he had been executed as an undesirable by the KGB. After all. You can't go saying these things about God and socialism on TV. At least you couldn't back then. But maybe it was less poetic. And more hurtful. Maybe he had gone to one of his other girls. Maybe he had positioned her on a tall flight of stairs. Much taller than the one that led to my apartment. Maybe he had hovered over her. Maybe he had looked down upon the vista of her limbs spread out in all the different positions. Maybe he had said to himself. This is the one. This is the one I could never grow tired of. Maybe they had fled together into another life. Maybe he had abandoned his baby. Maybe he had taken the plunge with someone else. Or maybe it was art. My father interrupted my thoughts. Maybe his life has become his art. My father said. And now he is done with it. Yes. My father said. Yes. And he marvelled at it. Then he said. He always had the edge over me. He was always one step ahead. God damn it. He said. It's perfect. What a performance. He said. And here's me. He said. Back to art. Back to figuring it all out. We could run away. I said to my father. We could disappear. Don't you see. He said. Don't you understand. The gesture has to be just right. He said. We are weighing our lives here. He said. You can't weigh your own life. I argued. That's why they say God has judgement. Our lives are in the balance. He said. What about that. That's more justice than judgement. I said. Okay. He said. Well. I have to do my life justice. I can't be less than my own life. It's too much thought. I protested to my father. What Jaco did was spontaneous. He didn't sit and plan out the justice of his life. No. My father said back to me. He came to the point where his life was acting through him. How can your life ever not act through you. I asked him. That puzzled me. Haven't you ever heard of bad conscience. He replied. And he picked up his guitar. Haven't you ever heard of Jean-Paul Sartre. I heard he was an existentialist. I said. That doesn't mean you need to be one. A man is shot from a bow. My father said. C. Did he mean the genitals. I thought to myself. A man is shot from a bow. He said. Towards what. I asked him. A minor. His fate. He said. E minor. His truth. But things get in the way. He said. Like what. I said. But I knew he would say mountains. C. Mountains yes mountains. He said. F. But a man can change his bearings. G. A man can adjust his flight. C. Through the air through the air. He sang. A minor. A man can sail through the air. E minor. With such grace. C. If only. He sang. If only. F. A man is shot from a bow. He sang. G. A man rises in an arc. But what if he falls short. I asked him. What if he hits the ground. C. A rainbow. He sang.

Through the water. I thought. A man and a woman can adjust their path through the water too. A man and a woman can walk through the fire. It's when you are brought back to earth. That's the problem.

My father took me to Jaco's apartment. It was on the corner of an old street with a wrought-iron balcony a few minutes from Kirov Factory in the snow and in the cold coming from the Gulf of Finland. The sky above. Vaulted. That cold the poets talk about is true. That sky too. Beneath the balcony in the snow and the poetic cold and the sky like a great terrible vault holding it on their backs were two stone elephants. I'm reading this like a book. I said to myself. There were large bay windows. Reflecting the end of the day. Portals. Passing through. By this point I was interpreting everything. From the other side of the road we could see into the apartment. It was completely empty. A vault. A cold grey vault in the snow. Except for a dreamcatcher in the window. My father pointed out. And a bongo drum in the kitchen. He said.

I took photographs of both of them. It was like a crime scene. Spectacular. My father said. Look at that. He said. What a disappearing act. He said. This is like an installation. He said. This is greater than anything in a gallery. He said. Then he took me for an ice cream.

Do you think that when a life is realised it gets cut off. I asked him. By God. Or by the fates of realisation. Who are the fates of realisation. He asked me. I made that up. But you know what I mean. I said. We're here to achieve something. I feel sure of that. He said. I had a scoop of vanilla pod and a scoop of coffee cream. What am I here to achieve. I asked myself. What are you here to achieve little one. I asked my baby. And where does it all end.

And why. Questions like that. Was mother fulfilled. I asked my father. Was mother at an end. What did she achieve. She achieved you. He said. But if everyone has to achieve everyone else. Then things will never end. Things end and they begin again. My father said. That's how things begin. Through endings. What did Jaco say on TV. Birth and rebirth. Do you think Mummy could be reborn. I asked my father. I put my hand on my stomach. I held my baby. I think my father saw me. I think I'm pregnant with Mummy. I said. At first my father looked at me like that. What. Then he thought that I was making a joke. That's funny little one. He said. That's funny. We'll all end up as our own mothers and fathers at this rate. He said. Then he made an announcement. I'm getting back into music. He said. I'm putting on a final show. For Xstabeth. He said. I have it all worked out. He said. Then he ordered a coffee. I'm booking the same venue. He said. I'm going to work out a series of songs. But I'm not going to ask to have it recorded. I'm not going to ask to have it out on LP. I'm going to leave it to the fates. He said. You mean the fates of realisation. I said. He laughed at that. I want to see if she is still true. He said. And I want to prove my love for her. Then maybe we can disappear. Baby. He said. Then he stroked my face. I thought about Xstabeth. And what I could achieve for me. But also who was this ghost saint in the face of the real world. And I thought about paying attention. And how you can miss the target completely. Without even realising.

XSTABETH

isappearing isappearing

xstabeth isappearing

xstabeth

isappearing

quiet the one

one isappearing

(   )

(   )

(.................................. n)

(.............. on)

(.......................one)

((reflectione))

(...................... one)

(.............. on)

(................................... n)

(   )

( )

I am

(softe stone) (serene)

(moone rackte) (visione)

I

isappearing isappearing

xstabeth isappearing

xstabeth

isappearing

quiet the one

one

isappearing

you may compare me to the moone

you may stare still moone

little moone

you may stare that a snowflake is an reflectione

if you like perhaps is as suiteable

they must stare

the girls

for miles go the girls oone

an up

yonder yurroughe

be the name

oone

an up

O

oone

where us girls go

up

upone canale

little ones be still gainste

tieme!

upon the tip of the tongue you are the highest

stare still

comaneth your creator!

O

let me look at you from another whorl what vision

I am overcome

with the beauty of the softe stone I place insize you

moone rackte

is what you are to me

still stare

now stand

visione

isrobing

isislence

islence

isappearing

quiet the one

one isappearing

B ut first we took a holiday. And on top of that I had an affair with a dastard. With a dastardly man. We took our first holiday together since mother had died. The first holiday we had taken since mother had died on her holiday. But that was a different holiday. We went to the home of golf. We went to St. Andrews. In Scotland. We flew to Edinburgh Airport. Which was covered in fog like an old ballad. Then we drove through the fields of Fife. My father and I. And our secret baby. Which didn't look so secret anymore. But which I covered up by eating ice creams. You're getting fat. My father said. As we drove in the car. My father had no tact sometimes. Lucky for me. You're fat when you're happy. He said. We took a hotel on The Scores. With a view out to sea. There was a golf tournament taking place.

Every morning we would get up. Then we would take our towels and lie on the beach. My baby was kicking more strongly now. So that I began to feel funny vibrations running up my spine. My spine where it had tried to heel me backwards. Don't babies normally kick from the front. What did I know. But I couldn't help getting the feeling.

The feeling that it was turning me backwards. That my
baby was pushing me into the past. I looked at my father
on the beach. Standing in the water with the soft waves
lapping. Lapping around his legs and with his dark trunks
on. His dark trunks with the white pull-string. His hair
like a Fifties rock 'n' roll star. And the people in the
background. Running into the sea. And already it was like
an old yellowed photograph. Already it was like all the
colour leaking out of the world. Then my father would
take notes. He would sit on a towel on the beach. Just as
if he was sitting in the past. In another holiday altogether.
That's how it felt when I looked at him. It must have been
all those goodbyes. I told myself. He would sit there. Or
he would sit on a bench. Just above the beach. A bench
where he could see me. From a distance. A bench where
it must have appeared that I was in the past. That I was a
photograph. With all the colour leaking out. And he
would write. He was working on lyrics. He said. But
when I sneaked a look at his papers. When I opened his
bag when he was in the shower. It was mostly drawings.
Drawings like this. Let me see. Like this ∧.∧ or like this
~.~ or like this ∩.∩ or like this «.». And that's when I
realised. He was drawing birds. He was sitting at the
beach and he was drawing birds. Like a little child. Now
there are a lot of birds to draw in St. Andrews. That was
understandable. Gannets and terns. Oystercatchers and
fulmars. Pied wagtails and greenfinches. Warblers and
fieldfares. But most of my father's doodles. They were
doodles if I'm being honest. Most of them looked like
gulls. Like gulls flying in from the sea. Which was his

vantage point. Of course. On the bench and on the
beach. Of gulls returning. Coming back. That's how it
seemed. Gulls crossing oceans to come back home. This
will be a good start. If he can sing this at the concert.
That's a love song. I thought. That proves it right there.

My father had bought us tickets for a golf tournament. It
was the first time we had seen it in real life. We had seats
on the stands. On the high stands. No one told us that it
was impossible to see the ball. That the ball was so small.
And so white. So white against the landscape. Invisible.
Especially from the stands. We had been used to seeing
the golf on TV. Where the camera follows the ball. God
only knows how. That's a real skill. Because in real life.
From the stands. It was impossible. And of course
fascinating. It was like acting. Or mime. Where in the sky
was the ball. The players would walk up in front of the
stands. And everyone would applaud. They would walk
up in smart black tank tops and gloves. And they would
wave. A casual sideways wave to the fans. That was us.
Then they would survey the land ahead. Everyone was
silent. Except for the gulls that my father drew. Everyone
was silent as they surveyed the vista up ahead. Everyone
was silent as the land came to speak. Vista. Everyone tried
to listen. Everyone tried to listen to things like dog-legs
and bunkers and fairways. And of course rivers. Small
rivers. You can see why this would appeal to a Russian.
Or a novelist. Or a Russian novelist in particular. The
fairway. The blank canvas. The page. The always up
ahead. Like in a Russian novel. Faith. Faith in the future.

Faith in the up ahead. And awe at its construction. And
the relationship of everything with everything else. Up
ahead. When you arrive there. And the small part you
played. In its construction. Up ahead. Yonder. Even as
playing is effortless. Golf.

Then the golfer would touch their hat. Not their hat.
More like a visor. They would adjust their visor. Then
they would have a talk. They would have a talk with their
caddie. Talking wasn't forbidden in golf. Quiet talking.
Confessions. You would imagine. Confessions of nerves
and confusion as to what lay ahead. A nervous joke. Perhaps. My father and I were sure we witnessed several of
them. Then the reading of the grass itself. The squatting
down and the laying out of the club on its side. What are
they doing. I asked my father. Taking the lay of the land.
It is called. He said. You can take that. Wow. Then there
was the approach. The approach to the ball. Which
involved the caddie laying down the golf bag at a
particular angle. Then putting his hands in his pockets.
Golf is a two-man sport. I realised. Then. Then the golfer
approaches. He imagines the flight of the ball through the
air. He imagines moving while not moving. Which is
swinging. He makes calculations. He wets his finger
sometimes. And puts it up to the air like a ship's captain
maybe. He practises his swing. Next to the ball. Next to
the ball so close he almost dislodges it. Why so close. It
has to seem real. My father said. Then the golfer looks
down. He has internalised the landscape. My father told
me. He now feels it inside. He looks down. He will not

look up again until the ball is in flight. He adjusts his leg. His eyes run down in a straight line. He locks his body while keeping it loose. How does he do that. In that moment he is perfectly in tune. What is perfectly in tune. Everything. Corpuscles. Lungs. The soft triangles at the back of the eyes. The cool flesh. The faint electric charge that the flowers next to the fairway give off. The impossible flight of a bee. His cream slacks. Golfers wear slacks. That's another thing. The perfectly creased slacks. Everything and nothing counts. Everyone holds their breath. Except for the golfer. It is important that he does not obstruct his breath. What is perfectly in tune. Then he swings in a perfect arc. Like Michelangelo or Da Vinci. Watch the toe of his right foot. How delicately it stands on end. Tiny toes. The ornate white shoes are tough and delicate. The impact makes a satisfying noise. Like hard bubblegum. The ball disappears into the air. It is eaten by the air. It is confused by the sky. Which in St. Andrews is pale white and blue. Everyone looks. Everyone's eyes scan faster than ever before. Everyone's eyes attempt to follow the arc. Everyone estimates then follows through. Everyone repeats the actions of the golfer in their own mind. But sees nothing. Where will we end. The golfer too. It has to be imagined. He often sees nothing. He goes on faith. That what is up ahead is exactly as visioned by him. That he has set the future perfectly in place. But a reaction is required. A hand is brought up as if to shield the eyes. From the soft sun. It becomes like a mime. Just as in the theatre. Small actions are amplified. Exaggerated silent discussions take place between the caddie and the golfer. The headshakes. Whether in doubt or amazement. Elsewhere there is a reaction. Distant applause. He is still on the fairway. A good golfer you would imagine could detect the subtlest impact. But everyone is playing at once. There are many golfers on the one course. Playing through. They call it. Many subtle impacts. Up ahead and way behind. And many balls too. A confusion of golf balls. Which is why there are people up ahead. To bear witness. Golf balls in a certain position. It occurs to me they can be read themselves. What is the lay of the land. The balls have been cast. The balls have been cast as if through an invisible curtain.

And what of the walk. The walk afterwards. There is no victory walk in golf. It is always part resigned. Part resigned and part nonchalant. The walk is part of the performance. It must have style. Even when walking into the invisible. The impossible to predict. This isn't chess. This is more like writing. Always starting from scratch. On the blank sheet. Always beginning again. Even when you think you've cracked it.

But maybe not. Because we went to a reception afterwards. In the Old Course Hotel. My father got us tickets. There we met a famous golfer. Is it blank. I asked him. Is it invisible up ahead. You can see it. He said. You can see it when you follow through. He said. What does that mean. When you go through the ball. He said. Once you hit it and you have followed through you know where the ball will be. What it will do. You mean you can tell

the future in the present. Almost. He said. But not quite.
You read your own body. It's like. And that implies a
place up ahead. A position. Can you read the other
bodies. That's irrelevant. He said. In golf you are playing
against yourself. My father asked him a question. Are you
always in command. Do you not have to let go. There is
only so much. He said. Only so much positioning. Only
so much thought. Then it's in the lap of the gods. My
father nodded at me. This is art. He said. Can you play
golf at night. Of course not. The famous golfer said.
That's ridiculous. But after what he said why. Then the
famous golfer invited us to a party. There is a party at our
hotel in The Scores. He told us. Why not join us later.
Why not.

Afterwards. After the golf was over. But before the party
had started. We walked round the links. Why do they call
golf courses links. Links in a great chain. One invisible
shot into the future. One random position. Never to be
repeated. And then the next. How do you link them
together. How do you make sense. At the hotel there were
men. And there were women. Mostly dowdy women.
Golfers get groupies. My father said. Just like a rock show.
Only with less make- up. The party had spilled out onto
the street. The golfers and the women and the fans were
standing around tables outside the hotel. At the
bandstand across from the hotel a Scottish pipe band
were performing. In full Scottish regalia. Some golfers
began to sing along. Some Scottish golfers. No doubt.
And some Americans. About a flower that bloomed in

Scotland. Once. The sun was orange. And luxurious. And smouldery. It was an evening for romance. And for drunken nostalgia. The famous golfer saw us and made his way over. I played bagpipe music to my unborn baby. He said. Why did he tell us that. It's good for them. He said. Drone music makes brains grow in peace. He said. Drone music. My father said. Do you like The Velvet Underground. He said. Lou Reed. Never heard of them. The famous golfer said. Golfers have poor taste in music. I learned. Except when it's pre-natal. Then expect anything. The only thing my father and the famous golfer could agree on was Steely Dan. What do you think of St. Andrews. My father asked the famous golfer. There are whores everywhere. He said. It's unexpected. I mean in a place like St. Andrews. He said. This was a surprising comment. He was famous enough to be able to steer the conversation. I realised. Famous enough to steer it somewhere else without question. Plus. He was drunk. There are streetwalkers everywhere. At night. He said. Haven't you noticed. Where. My father asked him. We were new to town. He explained. On The Scores. He said. They don't call it The Scores for nothing. He said. Do you like whores. The famous golfer asked my father. Oh yes. He said. My father who was also drunk by this point. I love whores. He said. I felt like I might as well not be there. But then I felt like the whole conversation was directed towards me. I felt like a tennis ball between two men again. But this time like a golf ball. Russian whores are the most beautiful in the world. My father said. It's hard to disagree. The famous golfer agreed. They fly whores in for the golf in St. Andrews. The famous golfer said. There are opportunities for everyone. That was obviously aimed at me. I thought. Anyway. He said. Who likes vodka. We laughed and said of course. Even though inside we rolled our eyes. Some more famous golfers got so drunk that they danced on a table. Another one pulled up a woman's dress while he was dancing with her. To reveal black stockings. Do you believe in the saints. The famous golfer asked me. We were sat at a table on our own. My father was with another drunken golfer. Like St. Andrew. He said. Do you believe in reincarnation. I laughed then. This is a typical Russian chat-up line. You mean like St. Peter. I said. But the golfer creased his nose. His small plain nose. I mean it. He said. I think you go on and on forever. He said. I think that at some point you get to live every life. But how will you know it is you that is doing it. I asked him. Doesn't matter. He said. You is you. Always. Then he shrugged. Let's ask your father. He said. Father. He shouted. That's what he called him then. Father. He said. Do you believe in the saints coming back forever. He said. My father came over drunk. I'll tell you about the saints. He said. Does anyone have a guitar. He asked the room. Now we're talking. A drunken golfer said. Someone produced an acoustic guitar from behind the bar. My father sat down on a stool. The room became silent except for some women and men who picked up their drinks and moved outside. My father began to pick at the strings. In a hypnotic style. One bass string. Up and down. One bass string. Then he began to sing. He began to sing like an old man. From out of the past. The lives of

the saints. He sang. E minor. They're awful funny. E
minor. They're awful funny. He sang. They're awful funny.
Take the saint that hung on. He sang. E minor. Take the
saint that let go. E minor (droning). They're awful funny.
In their way. He sang. E minor. Take the saint that woke
up. He sang. That woke up to himself. One day. He sang.
E minor. Now isn't that funny. He sang. E minor. And he
looked around himself while he sang. The lives of the
saints are awful funny. He sang. They're awful funny.
They're awful funny. Then he played an unaccompanied
solo. On the high strings. An unaccompanied solo that
sounded like ascending a high tower. On a spiral staircase.
Then throwing yourself off the top. The sun sinks into the
quiet sea. He sang. E minor. The sun sinks into the quiet
sea. E minor. The lives of the saints are awful funny. He
sang. They're awful funny. They're awful funny. Some
people applauded. Some people laughed. Awkwardly.
Some people stared out of the window. Into the thin air.
Into the last of the sun. Into the sea. Then everyone went
back to talking and drinking. She's with me tonight. My
father said. As he handed the guitar back. She's with me
tonight. He said. Inevitably he found a knife somewhere.
He suggested a game. But no one wanted to play. This
isn't Russia. I told him. This is St. Andrews. Exactly. He
said. It's the home of the saints. What's wrong with these
people. He said. Don't they have any belief. Besides. The
famous golfer said. We all have to play again on Monday.
He said. We need to keep the head. You call yourself
artists. My father spat. Then he went outside and smoked
a cigar on the steps. The famous golfer. Who smelled of

old aftershave and of sun cream. The famous golfer who
wore a short-sleeved two- button shirt. The famous golfer
who had sandy hair. I don't want to give too much away.
You would know him. He's a famous golfer. The famous
golfer who I could see had a semi-erection through his
slacks. He came up to me. He whispered in my ear. I want
to fuck you up the arse. He said. I want to do you up the
shitter. That's what he said. I thought about how golfers
sense the lay of the land. I thought about how flowers
send out electric signals. Follow me. I said. I instantly
took command of the situation. Once more. I took his
hand and led him up The Scores. I led him past the castle.
I might as well have led him by his big erection. Through
his slacks. I led him down the stone steps. I led him down
to the small beach next to the castle. I led him over to
where there were the remains of a fire. Still smouldering.
Then I dropped to my knees in front of him. I dropped to
my knees and looked up. With an expectant expression.
Call me daddy. He said. Okay daddy. I said. Okay big
daddy. I said. What are you going to use on me. I said. I
was making a joke about golf clubs. But he didn't get it.
I'm going to use my big dick. He said. You'll end up in
the bunker. I said. That's the plan. He said. He got that
one. Then he just stood there. He's nervous. I thought to
myself. He can't take it out on his own. Allow me. I said.
He stood with his hands held behind his back. Like a
prisoner. Or like an admiral on the deck of a ship. While I
undid him. I want that big dick daddy. I told him. You're
such a big man. I said. I want that big rod. I told him. I
wasn't sure if I really did want it. But I was responding to

the situation. On top of that I was driving him wild.
You're a little whore. He said. As I licked him with my
tongue on the beach. On the beach next to the
smouldering fire. Looking up. Then he said. Now's the
time. Now's the time you little bitch. But he had no
finesse. Not so fast daddy. I said. You need to warm me
up. Don't you know. Don't you know. I said. And I
stroked his face. But he pushed my hand away. I know
what little bitches like you need. He said. I know you do
daddy. I said. I know you do. I kneeled on a rock and
pulled my panties down. Watch me daddy. I said. Look at
me daddy. I said. Then I inserted one finger in there. One
slow finger. And then eventually two. Okay daddy. I said.
I'm ready for you big daddy. Go in slow daddy. I said. Go
in slow and come out fast daddy. That's it daddy. You're
the first daddy. I said. You're the first to take me in the
arse. I said. It's all yours daddy. I used the word arse. The
arse with the hard r. Normally I would have said ass. But I
was echoing. Mirroring. He started mumbling under his
breath. Talking fast to himself. Words I couldn't make
out. Like a prayer or an incantation. A Latin incantation.
Then he said. You won't walk for a week. He said. For a
week you will be walking on tiptoes. He said. My little
arse on tiptoes. I said. I'll wear my stilettos daddy. I said.
I'll walk on my toes in my stilettos daddy. I said. He bent
over me. He put his arms beneath me. Round my belly.
Round my swollen belly. Secretly he held my unborn baby
in his arms. He bent over and without knowing. He bent
over and without knowing what he was doing. He held
my little baby in his arms. My little baby who for all I

knew might have been my mother. My little baby who
might have been my mother coming back. Like the saints.
Coming back from across the sea. And of course then I
remembered. Who knows what happens on a beach in the
dark. You know nothing. I remembered Jaco saying. You
know nothing. I said. I said it out loud. You know
nothing. That's right you little bitch. The famous golfer
said. That's right. He said. As he whispered in my ear.
While he finished me off. As he whispered in my ear while
he held my unborn baby in his arms. You're nothing to
me. You little bitch. He said. You're nothing to me. That's
right daddy. I said. You know nothing. You know nothing.
You know nothing. Then I came. I came like the girl in
the strip club came. Like I never knew you could come.
Like a huge echo inside me. Like a huge echo that comes
from all the way in the beginning. And then spills over
you like the sea. As the famous golfer held us both in his
arms and took us right back to the beginning.

Afterwards it was hard to explain. I knew without
knowing that we would have a holiday romance. That we
would fall into it. I had numbers in my head. Vague
numbers. Like fourteen days. Twelve nights. Sixteen
lovemakings. I felt it all up ahead like a birth or a
premonition. I was being kicked backwards again. That's
how it felt. I was being put in position again. I realised it
was like there was something in the future. Something in
the future that had to take place. And that needed me in
the past to do certain things.

You talked about the saints. I said. I said this to the golfer on our second date. Which my father knew about. But said why not. Why not. After all he is a famous golfer. You talked about the saints. Do you think they are as alive as ever. I'm not a religious man on the whole. The famous golfer said. I can see that. I said. And we both laughed. On the beach in St. Andrews. We laughed hard at that. But the saints are approachable. He said. Well. What exactly do you mean. Approachable. I mean you can come to them easily. I mean they are as alive as they ever were. They made the decision to stand out. As an example to others. An example of what. Though. An example of seriousness. He said. An example of reverence. An example of honouring life. He said. Is that what we were doing last night. I said. On the beach. In the dark. There are saints for everything. He said. Saints for flies. Saints for slugs and snails. Saints for gulls. He said. Saints for gulls on their lonely flights across the sea. Saints for arseholes. I said. Saints for arseholes that walk on tiptoes. That's me. He said. I'm the saint of arseholes in heels. What about whores. I said. You love them too. That's right. He said. That's right. I'm the saint of whores' arseholes in heels. If only I could tell you his name. He really said all this stuff. You would be amazed. But sorry I'm faithful.

My father and I are haunted by a saint. I told the famous golfer. A saint called Xstabeth. But what is she the saint of. The famous golfer asked me. Mmhh. I said. Fathers and daughters maybe. I said. Girls maybe. But also songs.

St. Andrews is the home of the saints. The famous golfer
said. You came to the right place. That's for certain.
Listen. He said. I have my own sainthood to think of. Do
you fancy a game. He said. Not if it involves knives guns
or golf clubs. I said. It's okay. He said. I'm not the saint of
those. The game was to whore me out. It's a dream of
mine. He said. It's my sainthood speaking. He said. Well.
I told you about positions. About vague numbers and
shapes in my head. Now I could see it coming together.
Now I could imagine my memories before I had even had
them. Like in golf. It will be perfectly safe. He said. We
will dress you up. He said. Then have you walk The
Scores at night. I will be there the whole time. In secret.
Watching. If anything happens I can break it up. But if
not I will follow you. I will follow you with your John. I
hate that word. I told him. Okay. He said. What will we
call them. Well. Why couldn't they be saints too. I said.
No. He said. Not yet. They might end up that way. Who
knows. He said. But not yet. I'll pick up worshippers. I
said. How about I pick up disciples. Okay. He said. You
take your disciples down to the beach. And let them have
their way with you. Holy Christ. He said. The thought of
it is driving me crazy. But not in the arse. He said. That's
the rule. I get the arse afterwards. The arse is the point.
He said. This is a real holiday romance. I told myself.
This is really free. I said to the famous golfer. I feel so
free. He said to me. I walked around St. Andrews in my
high strappy heels. With my arm in his. He bought me all
sorts of new clothes. Short skirts. And lingerie. And
expensive nylons. Everyone was looking at us. While we

shopped. I've always wanted to do this. He said. This is a dream to me. He said. I just never met the right person. He said. Nothing lasts forever. I knew that. So give me two weeks of a crazy dream. I said to myself. We're co-conspirators. I told him. We're Bonnie and Clyde. You're a perfect Russian whore. He said to me.

A Rainbow in Xstabeth
by Dorothea Wiggin (Dx(e))

A rainbow requires of us three things, three aspects, three perfect alignments. It requires of us the precise atmospheric conditions. Furthermore, it requires the presence of the sun, up in the sky. Finally, it requires the presence of ourselves, as observers, without which it has no one to present itself to. Without us, rainbows would be all aghast and forlorn, instead of presenting us with the marvellous sight of every colour hidden deep within the world in a triumphal arch whose endings are in fairy-tales and in lost kingdoms. But it also relies on precisely the right angle, precisely the perfect relationship, between atmospheric conditions, the lucky old sun in the sky, and dear old livelong us. It is true that rainbows have associations with the bow, and with archery, and with hunting, and with the hitting of a target. Because outside of the specific angle necessary to enter into communion with ourselves, well, where is it? Someone who is not in my position may doubt the reality of what I have seen. But I have seen this world and in its (*missing*) I have witnessed it disappeared of all but its colour. A rainbow requires of us three things.

By day my father worked on his notes. Which like I say were mostly drawings of birds. He would sit on a bench at the beach for hours. Looking out. And he would sketch and draw. Everyone who has ever come here. He said. Everyone who has ever come here thinks they see the same birds every time. In the same places. He said. The same bird is replaced by the same bird. He said.

Then at night I would have my rendezvous. I have a rendezvous with my famous golfer. I would tell my father. I would get dressed up. Like an overwhelming Russian whore. Then I would walk The Scores. I would walk The Scores in the strange blue half-light. Which is St. Andrews at night. In the summertime. And I would know that somewhere. Somewhere. My famous golfer was watching me. In secret. I would feel his eyes ravish me. I would feel his pulse race. As I stood under the light of an old streetlamp. As I made myself available to strangers. But first I realised that the famous golfer was wrong. There were no whores in St. Andrews. I walked from the hotels across from the bandstand. All the way along to the castle. Then from there down past the ruins. And around the harbour. Then all the way back again. And I never once saw a fellow whore. At first. At first I felt robbed. Then I felt relieved. I'm walking through a fantasy. I told myself. I am walking through a man's fantasy. The first night nothing happened. I walked for hours. I sat on a bench next to a cannon. And smoked a cigarette. Then I pulled up my skirt. And stroked my panties. I thought he might be there. Behind the walls of the ruins. In the shadows of the lane. Watching me. If a Russian whore gets herself off in the dark of St. Andrews and there's no one there to see her what sound does she make. Miaow. I can tell you that she miaows. Then I kneeled up on the bench. And I began to writhe. Like I was being taken by an invisible being. I put my fingers in my mouth. I slid them down the back of my panties. I pictured the night growing eyes. Growing eyes through lust. I pictured an eye coming out of the sky. On a great stalk. Then another. And another. Then I imagined I was copulating. I imagined I was copulating with the air itself (the denizens of the air). I felt like I was possessed. Who is there when we can't see anyone. And when we disappear to ourselves. I felt like I was going crazy. Going crazy with self-love. With no-self-love. I felt the air turn inside out. I felt my own eye grow out of the sky. Until I was looking with looking. I was looking with what I looked at. That's it. I was seeing myself. But from someone else. Which was also myself. Is this making sense. I was outside myself and deep beyond myself. And inside myself too. Which is to say I felt like a sign. A sign that means forever. And I felt a strange certainty. A strange certainty that every one of us is watched over. Is watched over by ourselves. Which is out there. As much as in here. And there's nothing that isn't part of us. That isn't part of God. And that's when I heard the footsteps. I heard the footsteps approach from out of the shadows. It was the famous golfer. Thank Christ you're all right. He said. I'm sorry I was late. He said. Then he saw me all unravelled. All ruffled up and in disarray on a bench. I had the most wonderful evening. I told him. I had the most wonderful evening with a disciple. I said. A gentleman disciple roughed me up. I told him. You little bitch. He said. You filthy Russian whore. He said. And he took me right there and then.

My father noticed the change right away. You're so perky. He said. The whole world is after me. I said. I can't help it. The whole world is out to seduce me. I told him. I'm such a little tramp daddy. I said. What are you on about little one. He said to me. The universe is in love with itself all the time. I told him. Otherwise no more babies would be born. Babies. I said.

By day we took trips. My father and I. We took a trip to Anstruther. Which if you want to know does have the best "fish suppers" in the world. We took a trip out to an island. An island that was like a boil in the sea. An island with steep cliffs that we climbed up. And with birds. Odd birds that didn't react to humans. Birds that just sat and stared. And acted nonplussed. About the arrival of other creatures. My dad said they are probably not used to seeing humans. That's what happened to the woolly

mammoths. He said. When humans crossed the Bering
Strait. He said. That's between Russia and America. He
said. For the benefit of the rest of the party. When
humans crossed from Russia into America that is. The
woolly mammoths barely looked up from their breakfast.
He said. They had no experience of man. And of being
hunted down for food. There were no men in America at
this point. And for clothes. You could feed a family. Or
more. On a woolly mammoth. But the mammoths just
stood there. They didn't even stop eating. There was no
need to. They thought. And of course they were right. At
first. The humans didn't simply run in charging. They
took note. They observed. Then they went off and talked
about it. The mammoths just shrugged. And looked at
each other as if to say I guess there's more to this
wonderful world than any of us knew. What next. They
shrugged. Then the humans came back with a plan. And
some spears. And killed a mammoth. Even then the other
mammoths must have thought. Well. That was weird. But
they had no concept of types. They thought that
everything only happened once. Everything that was new.
That is. Of course they knew the grass kept growing again
and again. They knew that trees sprung up into forests.
And that small animals given a chance would hitch a ride
on your back. But they thought new things were one-offs.
By nature.

By this time people were standing around my father. On
top of this strange boil in the sea. Even the tour leader
was interested. They all stood there listening. I said to

myself. That's a natural father. Right there. That's someone who teaches things. No matter what. I felt so proud of my father then. My father and his knowledge. But the mammoths didn't have knowledge. My father said. As if he could read my mind. Like lovers and family members and autistic people can. Or so they say. And I felt as if I was on display. Through my father. Reflected glory was everywhere. In other words. The mammoths didn't recognise a killer. A predator. He said. They didn't realise that this killing was going to be repeated. So even at first when the humans began regularly hunting the mammoths. At first they thought they were just like annoying flies. To be batted off. When you are trying to graze with your family.

And at this point the birds too. The birds too were standing round my father. With vacant expressions on their faces. They had no idea of type either. No concept of friendly fathers explaining them. The birds just sat there and looked at us like that. What. And when one got killed the others ran away. My father said. They ran away but they drew no conclusions. So the next time they saw humans they didn't react by running off in terror. And the humans moved so fast. Before the species had time to evolve. Before the species had time to evolve an instinctive reaction to marauding humans. They were all wiped out. All of the mammoths in America. Wiped out faster than evolution could keep up. You see with human beings evolution had outpaced itself. My father explained. A woman named Sheila. A woman with cute oversized glasses and long hair down to her waist. Sheila stood and took it all in. We will return to Sheila. After I take a look at the birds. After I take a look at the birds and I say to myself. No. I don't know if father is right after all. These birds look nonplussed. But in a different way. It's not that they're not used to humans. It's that they have seen it all before. Between humans and birds. I thought. Between humans and birds we've seen it all before. Thinking and flying. I decided right there. Thinking and flying are equal with each other. When it comes to evolution. Thinking and flying are the same thing. Then there was Sheila like I promised.

MEMORY IN XSTABETH (2)
by Frances McKee (Dx(e))

B ut there's more to be said about what makes
significance. Significance is the ghost in the (soft)
machine. Some might say God is the ghostly significance
in the heart of the (soft) machine. Some might say that
"we," i.e. "us," i.e. "the self" is simply an agglomeration
of memories, which makes the self more like a moth-eaten
sheet if you think about it. What about all that is never
remembered? Which, if you think about it, is most of it.
How much of yesterday do we even have today? Are we
less than ourselves as a result? Or is the self by definition
something that is diminished, something that can only
exist as a shadow of a totality?

We have named many of the body's processes but what of
the significance particle? Why do certain memories stick
with us for life? What set the synaptic fire? These are the
building blocks of what we call the little self, what we
come to regard as us, which is what remains. Perhaps
rather than see the self as diminished we must recalibrate
our understanding of ourselves as being everything that
we let go of. But it makes no sense, or little sense, more
appropriately, to say that the self is the sum of everything

we let go of and everything that remains. Rather the self is what we are able to extract from all that we let go of and all that remains. But all that we are able to extract is all that remains. So, again, all that we let go of cannot contribute to all that we are, except, perhaps, in an empty, symbolic way, which is the domain of certain bad poets and not scientists, though I confess that sometimes the line does blur, ha ha (insert more jokes about science and poetry here).

Sheila like I promised was five foot two. With cute white heels. And tight bleached denims. And cute oversized glasses. And long blonde hair hanging down to her waist. Just about. And with men's shirts. Like checked shirts on. Too big and tied at the waist in a knot. My father's name was Tomasz. But she called him Tommy. I had never heard that before. Which made him strange and sexy and personable to another woman. Oh Tommy. She said. That's amazing. She said that several times on the boat coming back. My father is becoming Tommy. I thought. He is regressing back to a life before me. Then I thought. That's what holidays are for. After all. Oh Tommy. I heard her say. You're mean. This was on the boat back as well. Which meant he had told her one of his mean jokes. I think.

Then we became four. We both met people on holiday. That was convenient. We would sit around a table and have adult discussions in the sun. Then we would go off and do crazy terrible things to each other. I maintained my night walks. My secret displays for my lover with a thousand eyes. Sometimes I would meet people. People would walk past me. And they would hesitate and stop and look back. A Russian whore in St. Andrews. Who would have thought. Who would have fantasised about it and made it real more like. That's the difference. We did. At this point in my life everything was coming true because it had to. I was in a great romance. And I was in a normal romance. And my father was in a normal romance too. And we were in the home of the saints. How pretty it all was. How serene a holiday. We took Sheila to the golf. The famous golfer got us an extra ticket. This time we were in the exclusive stand. There were other golfers all around us. Seated in the stands. Sheila took off her shirt on the stand and underneath she had on a bikini top. It wasn't correct behaviour. My father looked around all proud. I've got some wild women here. I could see he was thinking. The famous golfer was doing well. It looked like he could win. He was neck-and-neck with another golfer. Who was more famouser still. Sheila stood up. In her bikini top. And shouted out his name. This was as he walked up the fairway. She shouted his name and then she shouted go go go. She had no idea that this was the most ridiculous behaviour at a golf tournament. This girl is naive. I said to myself. I'm a collector of naivety. Afterwards we had a meal at a restaurant on North Street. The famous golfer had to attend some kind of event. So it was just the three of us. My father was trying to get Sheila into good music. You need to get into the classics. He said. Don't you know Leonard Cohen. He said. It just sounds depressing to me Tommy. Sheila said. It's not depressing. My father said.

It's deep. You've spent too much time in the shallows. He said. Besides I don't really like music Tommy. Sheila said. You don't like music. My father was amazed. Is she for real. What do you like. He said. Sheila sat there for a moment. Like she had never really thought about it. Then she said. I like squid. That's what she said. I like squid. I could see that my father was head over heels. Then she said that she liked fairies. I like fairies. She said. What. We both said. You know. She said. The little people. The little people that dance at the bottom of gardens. Or in secret spots. And get up to all sorts of mischief. You've seen fairies. My father asked her. Oh yes. She said. Ever since I was a little girl. Ever since I was a little girl I've had a relationship with them. That's the word she used. She said she had a relationship with fairies. I think I was given to my parents by the fairies. She said. Because I was too big. I think I might be half fairy myself. She said. And then she laughed. That's impossible. My father said. There are no half fairies. What. I said to my father. What are you saying there are only full fairies. There are no full fairies and there are certainly no half fairies. My father said. This is childish superstition. Sheila just laughed. And then she burped. And then we all laughed together. There's a fairy tree not far from here. She said. There's a fairy tree in Craigtoun Park. We could all go and see it together. She said. All four of us. And if the fairies aren't around at least we can have a picnic. She said. Which resulted in the best day ever. But also the worst thing ever. Which meant the last of the best days. As you'll see when I tell you.

But the night before I went for my night walk. And nearly got picked up by a man. We all said our goodbyes. Then I got dolled up and sneaked out of the hotel. I headed for my usual route. Along The Scores. I scanned all around me as usual. Where was he. Where was my secret witness. Where was my famous golfer. I walked slowly. I liked the way my heels echoed up the lanes. And in through the gardens of the old houses like a sexy cat burglar. At points I caught my silhouette on the high walls. Like a weird old movie. Why does everything fantastic seem unreal. And that includes the past. Which gets more fantastic by the day.

As I was approaching the castle. As I was approaching the castle I spotted someone. Someone late at night. In the empty streets. He was walking as if to exactly intercept me. Is it my golfer. But no. We came closer. But the feeling was crazy. It was like two magnets fighting to stay apart. There was energy there. It was like when they say you are not supposed to meet your doppelgänger. Until the end. Even though from what I could see. Which wasn't much. From what I could see he looked nothing like me. He was a man for a start. But he was nervous too. He began to slow down. I imagined the famous golfer. Crouching down. Somewhere out there. This is what we had waited for. I was the bait. I was the delicious bait. I moved closer. He pretended to read the sign. The sign about the execution of martyrs. On that exact same spot. The past is getting weirder. I thought. Are we out of time. I thought. It felt like there was a force field between us.

Or an invisible fence. He looked at me from the side. He
read me like a book. I felt. I took a cigarette out of my
handbag. I went to light it. But first I put my finger out
into the air. I put my finger out and I touched the air
between us. And it rippled. It sent ripples out through
the air like water. Then the ripples froze. The ripples
froze like a sign in the air. Like circles within circles. So
that it appeared almost as if I was looking down a tunnel.
A tunnel that linked one moment to the next. A futile
tunnel. I thought. And I felt wretched and terrible. There
was a tunnel between us. A tunnel through the air. I
began to shake. My feet wanted to take off on their own.
This isn't supposed to happen. I told myself. Or is it. But
it could. I forced myself to stand my ground. The man's
head began to turn. To turn towards the tunnel. He
moved closer. We were next to each other. We were in
each other's space. We were far too close. How could we
be so close but still say nothing. How could we be so
close without touching. I felt like any closer and we
would shoot off like supernovas away from each other.
Like we were charges. Like we were forces. Forces
opposed to each other. The tunnel began to vibrate. The
moment was closing. I turned away and began to walk. As
calmly and as forcefully as I could. Away from the
moment. From the strange vortex. The man didn't move.
At first. Then he turned and walked straight through the
tunnel. The tunnel that had separated me from him. Now
he seemed more solid. More real. He began to pursue me.
Where are you my famous golfer. He began to pick up
pace. He was fast approaching me. The stranger was fast

approaching me. With a sense of decision. His walk was
decisive. He thought I was leading him somewhere. No.
This is the wrong rendezvous. I knew it. I cut through a
gate into the university buildings. But before I did. Before
I did I leaned over and took off my heels. And then I ran.
I ran through the mist in my stockinged soles. Through
the mist that was lying low over the grass. I ran through
the grass that was damp with dew. And I never left a
footprint. I looked behind me and I could see that I was
leaving no trace. I ran up and up. As if I was climbing
into the air. And then I saw the scene from above. I saw
the scene from above like in childhood when you have the
ability to fly. I floated up above the buildings of the
university. I floated up over St. Salvator's Chapel. Then I
hung there. Suspended in space. In the silence of St.
Andrews. In the deep blue sky. I saw my pursuer. He
came to a stop below me. He came to a stop and began to
look all around him. He looked in the bushes and
beneath the fire escapes. But he never once thought to
look up. And I could see the famous golfer. The famous
golfer as a black shadow. Making its way down The
Scores. In pursuit of my pursuer. I watched them like two
tiny pulses. Like two sluggish heartbeats. Sending blood
through the veins. One after the other. Two tiny pulses.
Before the lights go out.

* * *

At the park in St. Andrews. At the park in St. Andrews
we couldn't find the fairy tree. The fairy tree was on a

map. An old painted map. But in reality it was long gone.
Your fairies have moved out. The famous golfer said. He
was with us that day. All four of us were there. They
chopped down the fairy tree. Sheila said. Oh my. But then
we found something else. I've no idea how we found it. Is
it even there today. We found a fairy den. It was in the
trees. Hidden among the trees. It was the famous golfer
who found it. The famous golfer who today smelled of
sweat. The famous golfer who had sweat stains under the
arms. Under the arms of a short-sleeved striped yellow
shirt. You'll like this. He said. As he emerged from the
trees. After looking for a place to go. You'll like this a lot.
He said. Do you like toadstools. He said. I'm guessing
you do. He said. Do you like toadstools all gathered
under tents made up of wild witchy branches. He said.
Toadstools that fairies use to sit on. He said. Then he
took Sheila's hand. Yes please. She said. In a delicious
voice. He took her hand and they disappeared into the
trees. My father and I looked at each other. Is it another
tunnel. From one moment to another. Then we followed
after them. It was a true fairy den. Hidden among the
trees. There were ceramic painted toadstools. Painted red
with white spots. Gathered in circles here and there. Big
enough to sit on like stools. There were witchy dwellings
all made up of twisted branches. There were tall trees
with bare limbs stretched out and with bark like old
women's faces. And there were smaller toadstools. All
gathered together. Smaller hand-painted ceramic
toadstools. That looked as if they had been painted by
someone who was half blind. And the light was coming

through the branches. The light was coming through the branches and the leaves like the bottom of the sea. Anyone want a can. My father said. Then we all sat on a toadstool in the strange light. Hidden in the trees. We sat there and we drank beer. We were silent for a while. A blackbird landed on a branch and stared at us. This is magical. The famous golfer said. Eventually. What do you do back home. He asked me. He meant in Russia. Oh nothing. I said. I'm just a florist. Ah. He said. The weary flowers of time. I think the fairy den was going to his head. I didn't think a flower could get tired. Sheila said. Have you never seen a flower sighing in a breeze. The famous golfer said. My father was strangely quiet. That's the breeze that's making it sigh. Sheila said. That's not it sighing. That's like saying that's the sadness that is making you sigh. The famous golfer said. So you're not sighing. No. Sheila said. And she took off her sunglasses and put the tip of them in her mouth. Like an attractive librarian in a dumb movie. No. Sadness is not a physical thing that you can pass through like the wind. She said. Is sadness contagious. The famous golfer said. Can you catch sadness. Oh yes. If you're around it so much. Sheila said. I noticed my father then. In another world. Perched on a toadstool. Do they think they can catch sadness from my father. What star sign are you Tommy. Sheila asked him. As if she knew too. I'm a Scorpio. He said. I'm all Scorpio. He said. I'm triple Scorpio. He said. That's some heavy water. Sheila said. The scorpion that stings itself. The famous golfer said. You're good in bed. Sheila said to my father. But I knew that already. My father blushed at

that. He was cute as he looked at me. How come
astrology is true. Sheila said. How come it is so true but
no one can explain it. Then my dad spoke up. Finally. It's
something coming down from the stars. It's a quality of
light. He said. It's the quality of starlight and all that it
passes through and picks up on its way. At the moment of
birth our thin little skins are no protection against it. Our
thin little skins are no protection against fate. I put my
hand on my little baby. Do you think it is all written. The
famous golfer asked him. Do you think even the golf
tournament is written already. Do you think God has
fixed it. He said. And everyone laughed. I think it's
intricate. My father said. I think it's delicate. I think it's as
delicate as a woolly mammoth falling to its knees in the
Holocene. Is a Holocene like a hologram. Sheila asked
him. Kind of. Do you think I've already won. The famous
golfer said. Only if right now I crown you with a can of
beer. My father said. In the kingdom of the fairies. He
said. That's vital to your success. Then he shook up a can
of beer. He balanced it on the famous golfer's head. Then
he cracked it open. The famous golfer stood up slowly.
He stood up and walked around with the can of beer
balanced on his head. Foaming all over his face. And with
his arms out wide. And we all sang "We Are the
Champions."

* * *

You know how you have places in your mind. Do you. Do
you have places in your mind. Aren't you haunted by

places. By places you have never been to. I mean. By
places that you come upon. Places that have been there.
Inside you. All along. For instance. There is a seashore
inside me. A seashore that I have never visited. But that I
expect to visit one day. A seashore with clifftop houses.
With tall coloured clifftop houses. And with a wide
expanse of green grass. A wide expanse of green grass
that runs from the houses to the top of the cliffs. Where
there are walkways. Wide walkways. Where gentlemen
escort ladies in the late afternoon. It's an old-fashioned
seashore. Perfectly preserved. I almost said pickled.
Pickled inside of me. But not quite. Although it does wait
there. Perfectly preserved. The grass is untrodden. And
perfectly green. The houses are painted in pastel shades.
In peach and baby blue. And all the men wear hats.
That's still somewhere in my future. I think. Though it's
inside me right at this moment. Right at this moment. On
the promenade. Gentlemen are walking their sweethearts.
As the evening draws in. They're walking arm in arm.
And making delightful small talk. In front of the tall
happy houses. In full view of the sea.

When I first saw the Dutch Village. When I first saw the
Dutch Village at Craigtoun Park. In the middle of the
lake. With the small boats. With the small boats and the
swans all around it. I recognised it as something that was
inside me already. The single bridge leading in and out.
The overgrown children's play area. The deep water all
around and the reeds that grew up. The high white
turrets against the blue of the sky. The quiet of the

crumbling brickwork. The low arcs beneath the single bridge. The small boats passing through. The secret overgrown island. Father. I said. We have to take a boat out. My father and I hired a pedal boat. Sheila and the famous golfer took another. We were already splitting up. Going back. It was obvious. We pedalled slowly. Past the families and the children that circled the Dutch Village in the sun. Stop pedalling. I said to my father. Let go and stop pedalling. I said. And we began to spin in a tiny circle. Without a sound. Down below the silent water was thick with plants. With reeds and with grass that sighed in the water. That sighed and that fluttered and that waved in the water. Look father. I said. Look. It's the changing forest. Beneath us. Look. We are flying over the changing forest. Together. Will we ever remember. I thought. And I held my father's hand. I held my father's hand as Sheila and the famous golfer floated towards us. Across the changing forest. I smelled his smell. The smell of my father. As the famous golfer took out a camera. As he took out a camera and told us to smile. To smile for the camera. As he went to capture the moment. I thought. I thought what is there to hold onto. Even as I held my father's hand. His big hand. Even as I held on tight. Then the famous golfer fell over. He lost his footing as he went to stand up. And fell into the water. At first there was a panic. Someone jumped in to save him. But the water wasn't deep. The famous golfer reappeared stood on the bottom of the lake. It only came up to his chest. He stood there in the water for all to see. In front of the Dutch Village. And people began to recognise him. People began to applaud. It's the famous golfer. They said. And people laughed and made jokes. I looked round at the scene. At the crazy scene all around us. It's so delicate. My father had said. So intricate.

The famous golfer went to change in the public toilets. When he came back he was topless. His chest had short blond hairs on it. I hope that doesn't give too much away. He stood there in the sunshine and he signed autographs. While he was topless. A young reporter was there. And he filed a story. About the famous golfer's good-natured response to falling in the lake. He also mentioned me in the article. He called me his girlfriend. He said I looked like Olivia Newton-John in *Grease*. But it was poor reporting. Because he failed to say whether it was like Olivia Newton-John at the start of the movie. Or at the end. So it left people guessing. But of course it was the end. With the black leather trousers. And the heels. Then the famous golfer clapped his hands. He clapped his hands and asked for mercy. Have mercy. He said. I'm here for a picnic with my friends. And to relax. He said. He took control of the situation very effectively. I'm going to love you and leave you. He said. Then he took my arm. And he motioned to Sheila and my father. Let's go. He said. And we made our way over to the other side of the park where we could be undisturbed. Fame must be a real burden. My father said. Who wants to be famous. Oh. It has its moments. The famous golfer said. I'll bet. Sheila said. Then we spread out a blanket and had lunch. We sat in some trees across the fence from an old haunted

house that used to be a maternity hospital. The famous
golfer told us. Now it's haunted. He said. Or so they say.
It wouldn't surprise me. Sheila said. When traumatic
things happen they leave psychic imprints. Imprints that
are hard to erase. She said. You know like a stillborn
child. She said. And of course. She looked at me. She
knew. I'm convinced. She knew. Women do. We'll be
ghosts soon enough. The famous golfer said. I don't think
he understood Sheila's concept. But for now let's get
drunk. He said. Sheila had brought a Frisbee. It was
funny to see my father in his black blazer and black shirt.
With a cigarette in his mouth. Jumping up in the air. And
throwing the Frisbee back and forth. Throwing it back
and forth with Sheila. Who was wearing cut-off denims.
And a bikini top. Did Leonard Cohen ever play Frisbee.
The famous golfer and I lay there and watched them.
Their voices were muffled. Like when you are young. And
all the adults are talking downstairs. And it's late. There
wasn't a cloud in the sky. I lay with my head on the
golfer's chest. His soft barrel chest with the blond hairs.
Do you remember your mum and dad. I asked the famous
golfer. It's getting harder. He said. It's getting harder to
recall them. I remember remembering them. He said. I
recall something about them that I once recalled. He said.
It's getting more precarious all the time. He said. Like it
was a tower that would eventually topple. Occasionally
people would walk by. They would walk by and point
from a distance. That's them. I heard some people say.
They meant the famous golfer and me. That's us. I
thought. What about your mother. He asked me. Where

is she now. Oh. She's dead. I told him. My father was
doing that thing where you throw a Frisbee under your
leg. They looked hazy in the sun. She got murdered. I
told him. I don't know why I said it. She got murdered on
her honeymoon. I said. I was twisting the facts for no
reason. Her partner put his foot on her head. I told the
famous golfer. And drowned her. I said. Geez oh. The
famous golfer said. What happened to him. Where is he
now. Who knows. I said. You're kidding me. The famous
golfer said. But I just shrugged. That's Russia. I said.
Anyway. He said. Sorry. Let's talk about the future. He
said. The near future. He said. For instance. He said.
What toppings are you going to get on your pizza pie this
evening. He called it a pizza pie. I could have swooned.
I'm going to get tomatoes and mozzarella. I said.
Counting it out on my fingers. I'm going to get tomatoes
and mozzarella and then anchovies. Anchovies and capers
on top. And then black olives. Black olives. The famous
golfer said. Now we're talking. That's what's called a
puttanesca pizza. I told him. Is that right. He said. Wow.
He said. Then I'm going to have your arse for dessert. He
said. Then he rolled me over and ravished me in the grass.
It's all yours daddy. I said to him.

* * *

My father had insisted on taking everyone out for a meal.
At the Old Course Hotel. Even though he couldn't really
afford it. A slap-up meal. He said. You only live once. Etc.
Even though we were already drunk we went for more

drinks beforehand. Then we showed up twenty minutes
late. The concierge looked at his watch. As if to chastise
us. But then he recognised the famous golfer and became
extremely fawning. He gave us a table with a view. Then
came the free wine. My father ordered fish. A fancy fish.
His favourite French-style dish. With cream and white
wine. And what have you. Are you going to order your
pizza pie. The famous golfer asked me. Of course. I said.
We already planned what's on the menu. I said. He
slipped his hand down the back of my leather trousers.
And pinged the elastic of my panties. Sheila ordered a
prawn cocktail. That was all. She was too cute. But my
father wanted to smoke. Excuse me. The concierge said.
Excuse me but this is a non-smoking restaurant. Excuse
me. My father said. Excuse me but we're with ___ _____.
He said the famous golfer's name. Even though he was
sitting right there. We're with ___ _____. He said. And he
nodded at the famous golfer. I'm sorry sir. The concierge
said. There are no exceptions. But my father insisted. He
was becoming belligerent. You want to smoke Sheila.
Don't you. He said. I wouldn't say no. She said. See. My
father said. As if that proved something. Then he leaned
over to the people at the next table. Do you mind if we
smoke. He asked them. I'd rather you didn't. A gruff old
boy replied. Then he got up. My father got up and began
going from table to table. Asking people if they minded us
smoking. By this point he was staggering. Staggering from
table to table. Pointing at the famous golfer. Arguing with
the diners and the servers. Then I remembered Jaco. I
remembered Jaco at the strip club. When the lights came

up. Staggering from one stripper to the next. The look of contempt on the faces of the strippers. The look of contempt and incomprehension. The same look on all the faces at the tables. I collect naivety. I told myself. But I couldn't deny it. It was pathetic. Father. I said. Please sit down. I didn't want to say it. I felt disloyal. It doesn't matter father. I said. We're all fine. We're okay with it. Isn't that right Sheila. It's all fine Tommy. She said. Thanks for trying. She said. It doesn't matter Tommy. It's okay. No. My father said. It does matter. This was supposed to be our big meal. He said. But when the concierge took his arm he didn't resist. I saw the servers apologising to people for the scene. As my father was led back to the table. No worries Tommy. The famous golfer said. It was worth a shot. But my father just sat there. He sat there and stared at the table. Then the food arrived. It was the worst thing ever. It pierced my heart. To this day it's the worst thing I can remember. Maybe you won't think so. But there was just something about it. They put the fish down in front of my father. His favourite French dish. This dish that he could barely afford. And he picked up the fish. He picked up the fish and he tore it in two. He tore it in two and he threw it back down on his plate. I looked at it. Torn up on the plate. Torn up and with the sauce gone everywhere. And that was when I realised. That was when I finally realised that no one will ever love me as much as I loved my father. Not even my baby girl. Who at that moment was alive inside me. But please. Let's not talk about it any longer. Because I can't stand to think of that fish even for a second.

ENNUI IN XSTABETH
by Patricia Waters (SR\SIF)

Although sad, Ennui is the most beautiful concept of, all. It is melancholy fallen from grace. It has been trivialised in the modern world because people have come to believe there is simply *no time for it*. Precisely because of its scale. It combines an epic world-weariness that could almost be German with a fleet, barely there quality that makes it feel like you're experiencing the interstices of the world, the waste ground of the world, the abandoned car parks of the world, the dirty windows of the world, the moment between moments of the world, the mindlessly-walking-towards- something-from-something of the world and that something—that space between one island of experience and the next, that blink-and-you'll-miss-it wasteland, that desert space—is a land known as Ennui.

Melancholy requires a vista, an aspect or, better still, a retrospect, a lovely retrospect. Ennui is a Western take on what intrepid Buddhist explorers term the Pure Land. They call the Pure Land Sunyata. In the West, Sunyata is most commonly experienced not in nature, not in isolation per se, but in desolation, more properly. Lucky

for us—well, lucky for any intrepid spiritual explorers—
the great towns and cities of the Western world are the
equivalent of spiritual assault courses for warrior monks.
Beneath great concrete motorways where abandoned
mattresses lie next to rusting shopping trollies and
pointless abandoned shoes, in the smell of burning tires,
the land of Ennui greets you, brave voyager. But in the
Western world the practice has become so serious, so all-
pervading, that it has made monks of us all. City-centre
bars and restaurants often function as portals into Ennui,
the Pure Land, Sunyata. Raise a glass in company, brave
seeker, raise a glass and drain it, but continue to hold it
up to your mouth. Gaze through the dirty glass, listen to
the incessant babble of your pointless friends, inhale the
rotten odour of the old men on the stools, observe the
empty cheer of the football supporters, run a finger along
the dusty bar top, cast an eye over the couple that hasn't
exchanged a word all evening, examine the dead animals
wilting for life on the white plates, the sad confectionary,
the condition of the peas, catch the eye of the woman
sitting opposite, smell the toilets, watch the insects feed
on the crumbs of pickled onion Monster Munch on the
floor, listen to the TV, talk about sport, pick out the stains
on the carpet. Ennui, brave soul, is just another word for
heaven.

PS: Except vague, post-modern Ennui, which is just
another word for hell.

Afterwards we went back to the famous golfer's apartment. An apartment he had rented with a small garden in Baker Lane. We drank some more. And everyone began to tell tales. Tales of their childhood. Which of course I didn't have so many. As everyone else. But when Sheila went to talk. When Sheila went to talk she was playing with a comb. She was playing with a comb and holding it up in front of her face. And rubbing it on her chin. While she spoke. She was really drunk. And telling some tale about her brother. About how her brother and a friend had coerced people into lying down on the ground and then tied them up. So that they could take turns leaping over them on a motorbike. They had dragged them up the fields. Sheila said. No one could believe it. Everyone was killing themselves laughing. What. It's true. She said. Then the friend tied them up and my brother Peter. My brother Peter leapt over them on his junior motorcycle. No. Yes. He built a ramp to leap over them. Then they had to go get some more. To increase the distance. Wait. The famous golfer said. You have to speak into the comb. He said. What. The comb. He said. When you talk you have to speak into the comb.

Like a microphone. Okay. Sheila said. By now I was
crying with laughter. Even my father was slapping his legs.
Sheila stood up and held the comb up to her face. So.
They had to go and get some more victims. Everyone
cracked up. She swayed back and forth as she spoke into
the comb. Like she was on a junior talent show. They
made one of the captives watch that the others didn't run
away. This was up in the fields. Then they came back.
They grabbed some kid off the street and dragged him
down a lane. Then they tied his hands and marched him
across the field. Of course everyone could see them from
the back windows of their houses. The windows that
looked onto the fields. And someone saw these kids
leading this other kid across the field. Across the field
with his hands tied behind his back. And they thought
they were seeing an execution. It's a gangland execution.
They said. When they called the police. They could only
see them from a distance. But even so. Even so they were
so small. What kind of gangland was this. *Bugsy Malone*.
The famous golfer cracked up at that one. And we went
along with it. We hadn't got *Bugsy Malone* in Russia at
that point. But we knew it was funny. Then Peter is
leaping over more and more people. In front of the ramp
are eight victims. Were they scared. I asked my brother.
No. He said. They seemed like they were into it. Actually.
He said. Then our dad came. He came running across the
field. Just in time to see Peter leap over eight helpless
children. He ran up to my brother. And grabbed him by
the shoulder. The kids on the ground just lay there. And
my dad says to him. That was some leap. By the way. Do

you think so. My brother says. Yes. He says. Now give me
your bike. Peter shrugs. He's getting his bike impounded.
But then my dad says. Tie him up. And he points to Peter.
Tie him up and add him to the pile. That's exactly what
he said. No way. Yes. No way. Yes. And my dad gets on
the motorbike. The mini motorbike. No. Now there are
nine children behind the ramp. Sheila leaned back. And
she held onto the curtains. While she spoke into the
comb. Now there are nine children behind the ramp. She
said. And my dad takes a big wide circle. Before he
approaches. He drives off into the distance and comes
back again at full speed. And he shoots over all the
children like a rocket. He overshoots and makes an
amazing leap. All the children get up and are cheering.
All the victims are pogoing up and down with their hands
and their feet tied in the field. Cheering my dad. And
before the police come. Before the police come he
releases them. He releases them and they all run off. Not
a single person grassed them up. Sheila said. And my
father turns to my brother. And he says. Let that be a
lesson to you. And then he walks off like John Wayne in a
cowboy movie.

But wait. My father said. It doesn't make sense. He said.
How did you know they said it was like a gangland
execution. How did you know that's what they said to the
police. Easy. Sheila said. And she picked up the comb
again. Easy. The next day an old woman came up to my
dad. And she said. That was some leap. By the way.
Yesterday. In the fields. She said. I thought it was a

gangland execution. At first. She said. And I went and
called the police. Sorry about that. She said. If only I had
known. She said. And my dad just patted her on the
shoulder. And he said. Let that be a lesson to you. What
is he talking about. The famous golfer said. And everyone
laughed. Sheila put down the comb. And she sat on my
father's lap. Who will ever know what daddies think. I
said. And everyone laughed again. But this time for their
own reasons.

* * *

The next day was the first omen. The next day where
before we went to see the golf. We went shopping for
LPs. Father wanted to get a copy of *Songs of Love and
Hate* by Leonard Cohen. As a present for Sheila.

But the night before I had a dream. I had a dream where
Jaco and The Snork were boasting about making up
Xstabeth. Boasting that they had made up the whole deal.
We took Tomasz to the cleaners. That was what The
Snork said. In the dream.

Then we were flicking through the LPs. Where would we
be without hate. My father said. Love and hate locked in
an embrace. He said. Cohen knew that. He said. Can't
have one without the other. Even the people who say they
love love. He said. Even they hate. They hate hate. He
said. With love and with hate. He said. That's what Sheila
needs to understand. And then I'm not joking. I'm not

joking when I say that I looked up at that exact moment.
That exact moment as my father was talking about love
and hate. About how they were both necessary. I looked
up and out of the window of the record shop. And I saw
Sheila walking with the famous golfer. Plus. A third
person. A third person with a deformity. I saw them
walking together. On the other side of the street. I was
sure it was them. Although it was raining. And foggy. And
the haar had come in from the sea. Which made visibility
poor. Which made everything seem ghostly and unreal.
Which made it seem like the famous golfer and Sheila and
the deformity were speeding like shadows. Speeding and
not talking. Not talking like they had somewhere to go.
You say that father. I said. I was shaken up. You say that.
I said. But it's much easier to be on the end of love. Than
on the end of hate. But no less necessary. Little one. He
said. I kept my eye on the threesome. I kept my eye most
of all on the deformity. No. It couldn't be. It couldn't be
The Snork. It couldn't be The Snork come to take father
to the cleaners. And then what do you think happened.
Can you believe it. My father pulled out a copy of the
Xstabeth LP. A copy of the Xstabeth LP in St. Andrews.
The original Russian pressing. But not the first Xstabeth.
Not his one. Not the authentic Xstabeth. But the forgery.
The fake. The one that The Snork had said was even
better. The one that was mere poetry. What the fuck. He
said. He said that just as the threesome sped out of sight.
And it had no price on it. The Xstabeth LP had no price
on it. It was like someone had hidden it there. Like
someone had come into the shop and secretly left a copy

there. Left a copy for my father to find. He spoke to the
assistant. What is this LP. He asked him. No clue mate.
He said. That's exactly what he said. Looks like a Russian
name to me. He said. My father corrected him. Xstabeth
isn't Russian. He said. You obviously know more about it
than me pal. The assistant said. At first he was quite rude.
How much is it. My father said. It doesn't have a price on
it. That's weird. The assistant said. That's unusual. Must
be a mistake. He said. Then he said. Do you mind if I
stick it on. Do you mind if I give it a quick listen. The
assistant said. If you must. My father said. And even
though he looked at him funny just then. Even though he
looked at him funny the assistant went ahead and put it
on anyway. It was those same lines. Those same lines
about the frozen river. About crossing the frozen river.
Floating across the shop and out into the frozen air.
Casting shadows on the walls. And floating up. Floating
up and hovering in the air over St. Andrews. Drawing us
back. Back into the future. It was all too much. Wow. The
assistant said. This is pure poetry. He said. It was like he
was there to do a number on my father as well. This is
pure loner. The assistant said. This is pure loner folk. He
said. What's that. I asked him. It's a genre. He said. It's a
genre of one. He said. And then he laughed. It's a genre
of one again and again. He said. That's what Xstabeth is. I
said. I know. The assistant said. That's what I'm saying.
I'm having this. He said. That is if you don't want to buy
it. He said. But my father just stood there. Or rather he
stood somewhere else altogether. Caught in a dream.
Coming back to him. Swaying slowly from side to side. I

imagined the famous golfer and The Snork. Playing the music. Making the music. I imagined them in slow motion. Behind smoke. Dolled up like demons. And I imagined Sheila miming the words. Miming the words in the most horrible way. Miming the words with the comb. Miming the words using the comb as a microphone. Mocking my father like an evil clairvoyant. Then my father said. It's yours. You can have it. Then he took my hand. Then we walked out into the haar. The tall steeples of the churches were lost in the fog. The ruins looked haunted. The fog lay so low that the towers appeared to begin halfway up. The cars drove off into oblivion. People too. Faded away. We headed to the East Scores. Then down to the harbour. Where we walked out as far as we could on the stone pier. At the end we came to a ladder. A metal ladder that reached up into the clouds. We climbed up. Through the clouds. We came to the top of a high stone tower. Looking back. Looking back we had lost all connection with the town. The stone pier ran off into oblivion. Now we were an island. Sealed off from the rest of the world. At the head of this tower. That was when we heard the music. The new music. The most elemental music. Ghostly music. Music that was barely there. At first you had to turn your head to hear it. You had to turn your ears to face a particular direction. Do you hear that. My father said. Do you hear that music. (Droning.) That sound. Do you hear that sound. (Droning.) It sounds like an angel. My father said. It sounds like an angel breathing out. (E minor.) Then another tone joined it. A tone that was so far away. But

that was inside you at the same time. (E seventh.) A choir.
My father said. A choir of angels. (Droning.) It's only
ships. I went to say. It's only ships lost in the fog. But then
I stopped myself. Then I realised. It's not out there. We
stood there. (Droning.) Staring into nothing. And
listening to less.

* * *

By the time we crossed back into the town. By the time we
crossed back into the town everything had changed. We
went for a coffee. We went for a coffee in a coffee shop.
In the toilet they had a map on the wall. A framed map of
the Old Course at St. Andrews. But now it was mapped
out like in heaven. Parts of it. The map claimed. Parts of it
were now known as the Elysian Fields. The Elysian Fields
is the heaven of the heroes. It's where the saints go when
they die. Oh father. Are we dead. I thought in the coffee
shop on Market Street. Are we crossed over and dead.
Then I saw the River Eden. I saw on the map that the
River Eden marked the very boundary of the golf course.
And that the whole town was now east of Eden. Father. I
said. Father. As I accepted a café au lait. Do you know
that Eden has appeared. Do you know that the souls of
the heroes are walking on the fairway of the Old Course.
Father. Even as we speak. Show me the map. He said. Oh
good grief. He said. Can it be true. We went into a
bookshop. We went into a bookshop in the fog. On
Market Street. All of the books had changed too. All of
the books now said that the Old Course was bordered by

the River Eden. All of the books said the Elysian Fields were on the golf course itself. Everything has changed. My father said. Everything has been rewritten. Little one. He said. She's playing. My father said. That's her thing. He said. She's playing with me.

Yes. Yes. I thought. I've been playing too. So I could understand it. Then I thought about the famous golfer and Sheila and The Snork. I thought about them in the fog. Sneaking around St. Andrews. She's playing with them too. I thought. She isn't even faithful. But I could understand that. It was all part of the story. Hadn't my father said so himself. It was all so delicate. So precariously balanced.

* * *

We went to see the final day of the golf tournament. We saw the famous golfer. We watched as he walked across the Elysian Fields. That's the Elysian Fields. I said. To a fat American sitting next to me. That's the Elysian Fields that he's walking across. I know. The fat American said. He squatted down. The famous golfer. He stood back up. He put his hand to his visor. He spoke to his partner. He tried to see ahead as best he could. He took out a club. He stared at the ball and at the ground. Then he swung into the future. This is too much. I said to my father. This is high drama. Then he disappeared. He disappeared across the fairway in the fog.

Afterwards. Afterwards we heard that he won. The famous golfer. I won't tell you what year it was. Otherwise I would be giving everything away. We heard he won. But he didn't call. He didn't show up at the hotel. My father sat outside at a table. Outside the hotel. With a view across to the beach. Across to the west sands. Where the sun was going down once more. So delicate. I took my usual walk. My usual walk even though there had been no communication. I walked along The Scores at night. I displayed myself. To no one. No one was there. But still. I could feel eyes on me. My own eyes. Watching me. My own eyes. Greedy. Taking it all in. I displayed myself on a bench. I made myself available. I looked the part. He had called me the perfect Russian whore. The famous golfer. Now I was lonely. Not me. But I mean the me that watched me. She was lonely as she watched. I could tell. Don't ask me how. I had just come to the point. That's all. Baby. I said into the night. Baby. I said into the empty street. And the echoing walls. And the ruins. Baby. Is there anything I can do for you. But nothing. There was nothing. I was a ghost now. I had died. Remember. Then I began to notice things. Things like shadows creeping over walls. Things like the silhouettes of birds on high walls. Things like flowers sighing. Things like the waves coming in. Things that would never be repeated. Things like the sound of my footsteps in the dark. At first I began to match it. I began to match the sights and sounds as I walked. I'm ghosting. I said. I'm ghosting. Then I just gave up. I just gave up and walked back home. Back to the hotel. On my own. Without even trying. And with

everything sounding and moving around me regardless.
What a feeling. To just give up like that. I even walked in
the front door. Past the golfers and the fans. All sitting
there. Me dressed like a perfect Russian whore. Perfect.
For the moment. I had come to the point.

I changed and found my father in the bar. On his own.
Where's Sheila. I asked him. She had gone on a day trip
to Anstruther. To sample their fish and chips again. But
she didn't call. Do you think she is at the party. Do you
think she is at the golf party celebrating with the famous
golfer. To the winner the spoils. My father said. He
reached out. He reached out and at this point he put his
arm around my shoulder. And he said. You and me.
That's all he said. You and me. He said. We can't set a
foot wrong. I said to him. It's impossible. Don't you see. I
said. But I was coming from somewhere else. Soon we
were getting drunk and the bar was lively. It's time to go.
I said to my father. But no. For him it was time to sing a
song. Someone brought him a guitar. And he played cover
versions. Cover versions while drunk. He sang songs by
Leonard Cohen. And by Nick Drake. Of course. And one
about nothing. One about nothing. Again and again.
About being born and going blind. And about how
loneliness was the most precious gift. And the only thing
that was worth remembering. In the morning we took the
plane back to St. Peters.

THE DEATH OF DAVID W. KEENAN IN XSTABETH
by An Anonymous Bystander

David W. Keenan was found, bleeding from the head, but still breathing, at the foot of St. Rule's Tower in the grounds of St. Andrews Cathedral, from where he had apparently hurled himself. This was October of 1995. It is not clear how long he had lain there for, as it was raining heavily and the smirr had washed in from the ocean, so visibility was poor and the cathedral grounds were deserted. Indeed, on discovery of the body it wasn't possible to see the top of the tower, which was lost in the clouds and the fog. There was a book in his pocket, I clearly remember that, because just after I discovered the body a young woman appeared, who pointed out that he did, indeed, have a book in his pocket. I offered to run to a phone box and call for help if the young woman would agree to stay with the body. I don't know why I keep calling it a body, it was still alive then—he, he was still alive then, David was. Who I didn't know from Adam. Who I didn't know, at this point, was a well-known local writer but also a crackpot, is what I've heard. As I ran off, I turned to look back and saw that the young woman was crouched down on the wet grass and leaning over him. I presumed she was tending to his wounds or caressing his crumpled body. But when I returned, she was gone. And the book was missing from his pocket. She turned him, I thought. She rolled him. And I almost marvelled at the resilience of women. I started speaking to the body. Maybe I call it a body because it was unresponsive. I was having a monologue, a reassuring monologue, with an unconscious, dying body. And then, I'm not kidding you, the clouds parted. Literally. And there was this great rainbow over the cathedral. This great rainbow appeared, and it started moving its lips, the body, this body, David, this body that I had been talking to like a small, scared child with no response started mouthing something. And then I realised he was singing. I'm disappearing, he sang, I swear to God, I'm disappearing, he sang, in this soft, mad voice like a gentle lunatic. And I realised he was dying. I kneeled down beside him and I put his head across my thighs. I'm disappearing, he sang. He couldn't look at me, his eyes were all over the place. But it was like he was laughing, and bleeding, and convulsing, with joy. Who's he singing to? I asked myself. And I looked out there. At this rainbow in this graveyard beneath this tower. She's out there somewhere, I said to myself. I guessed there was a woman involved. I thought about the resilience of women all over again. As he sang himself to death there, in St. Andrews in the rain. Because I heard he died in the ambulance. I heard he died on the way there.

At home he fell into a slump. He described himself as being like an animal. My father. Like an animal that had lost its footing. On a thin mountain path. An animal that had lost its footing and had nearly fallen. An animal that had lost trust. In itself. Or in the universe. He wasn't clear. An animal that had displayed a weakness. Who knows. A pack horse. Or a mule. Or maybe just a dog. I have to make it up to her. He said. I haven't been paying attention. He said. I have to win her back. He said. I have to play the concert. He said. I'm an apostate. He said. What. He took out his notebooks. His St. Andrews notebooks. His notebooks that consisted mostly of simple drawings of birds. And he began to work. To work on new songs. Aren't you just going to wing it. I said. It was kind of a joke. Aren't you just going to let the spirit take you. I said. That's what you did before. I said. No. He said. No. It has to be right. I need precision. He said. It has to be delicate. He said. He went to see The Snork. He went drinking at Snork's. Any word on Jaco. He asked him. No man. The Snork said. The rumour is that he is living in a commune in the Urals with three wives. And that he has taken a vow of silence. The rumour is he saw the light.

The Snork said. What does that mean. My father asked
him. Who knows. The Snork said. You know it when you
see it. I guess. He said. Bastard. My father said. What a
disappearing act. That should have been me. He said. But
I stumbled. He said. The Snork had no idea what he was
on about and just gave him another drink. How was St.
Andrews. The Snork asked him. We rewrote the book. My
father said. St. Andrews is heaven on earth. He said.
Sounds like fun. The Snork said. Then he went back to
flicking through his records. Any more releases from
Xstabeth. My father asked him. Would you believe we
found one of those LPs in St. Andrews. No shit. The
Snork said. No fucking shit. That's what he said. Then he
put on a song by The Seeds. "Where Is the Entrance Way
to Play." On an album called *Future*. Perhaps he's
widening his remit. He said. Not he. My father said. Not
he. She. Xstabeth is a she. I doubt it. The Snork said. I
seriously fucking doubt it. Unless it's a she with an Adam's
apple and a beard. He said. If you get what I'm saying. I'm
playing a show. My father told The Snork. Back in the
saddle. The Snork said. And then he put on an LP by Bob
Desper. He put on an LP by Bob Desper called *New
Sounds*. My father would always play it at home. I never
got out of the saddle. My father told The Snork. I'm
always working. Always taking notes. He said. Always
soaking things up. Bob Desper began to sing. It's too late.
It's too late. He sang. It's too late for the driver. Just Bob
Desper with this doomy guitar. In a room full of echo. You
doing your usual covers set. The Snork asked him. Cohen
and shit. He said. That's not my usual shit. My father said.

That's to keep the monkeys happy. He said. I'm going deep. He said. I'm dredging the bottom. He said. This time it's as serious as your life. He said. Dredging the bottom. He said. Of course I pictured the body of my mother. The body of Jaco. Dredged up on a beach. On a beach in the dark. Tangled up in guitar strings. Their arms and feet tied together. Oh God. I thought. What is happening to us. Are we really raising the dead. Is everything tangled. I don't buy it. The Snork said. Don't buy what. I don't buy the whole Bob Desper shit. He said. What. You mean the whole back story. My father said. The shit about him being a blind preacher. The Snork said. Bullshit. My father said. No man. The Snork said. You really buy that shit. He said. Damn right I do. There are pictures. There are pictures of Bob Desper. Bob Desper in the echoing studio. Alone. Sitting with a guitar. Singing into a microphone. And he has no eyes. That's how my father put it. He has no eyes. Could have been anyone. The Snork said. They could have used any picture that they found. Who's they. My father said. Record scum. The Snork said. Cynical collectors. People trying to big up an average LP. He said. Trying to turn it into a private press legend. He said. Christian psych. He said. You know the deal. The story I heard is that it was a bunch of record collectors who made the damn thing up. Trying to fool collectors. No man. My father said. There's too much documentation. Besides. There is another record. There's an earlier group. Doesn't mean shit. The Snork said. Besides. My father said. You can hear the blindness. That's what he said. All the time Bob Desper is singing. Rolling down life's highway. He sang. Said he's gonna do things my way. That was always a weird line. The Snork said. I always tripped over that one. Is that what you mean by hearing blindness. No man. I mean you can hear that Bob Desper has never even seen his own reflection. Yet he's travelling down a highway. He's singing about travelling down a highway. And about death lying on the highway. And you can tell. You can tell he has no idea what a highway is like. You can tell he thinks it's something that has a particular sound. And a particular feel on the skin. I mean of course he has never driven. A blind man behind the wheel of a car. Give me a break. It's too late. It's too late. Bob Desper sang. It's too late for the driver. You can't fake blindness. My father said. Yes you can. The Snork said. All you have to do is close your eyes. That's not blindness. Blindness is a state. My father insisted. How do you know. The Snork said. You know as much about blindness as Bob Desper knows about driving on the highway. He said. Playing the guitar is one thing that you can do when you're blind. I'll give you that. The Snork said. There are plenty of things you can do when you're blind. My father said. Just most of them slowly. What would it be like. My father said. What would it be like to never have seen. Are there any other famous blind singers. He asked The Snork. Roy Orbison. Was he blind. No. But I heard he was an albino. Stevie Wonder. Of course. He said. The most depressing music ever. He said. I know. Tell me about it. My father said. But he sings like he had eyes in his head. He said. Maybe he went blind. The Snork said. Maybe he saw for a little bit. That would explain it.

But that's what I'm trying to say. My father said. When
Bob Desper sings it is clear that he has never seen the
light. You can hear it. Funny thing to say about a preacher.
The Snork said. A preacher who never saw the light. My
father said. That's why it's so heavy. Imagine having only
seen the light through the dark. Eternity opens her gates.
Bob Desper sang. She cries out it's too late. And they both
sat there and listened. It's like the opposite of being born.
The Snork said. Okay. He said. You got me. Maybe
Desper is the real deal. But my father couldn't get it out of
his head. Light in darkness. He kept repeating. Sound in
silence. And then he went back to working on his music.

* * *

On the day of the performance I got up and made him his
favourite breakfast. Which was exactly the same as his
father's. A single orange. Which he sucked all the juices
out of. A single orange that he never bit. Then some black
coffee. And a big thick heel of bread. With cheese on.
Then he said he was going to do some yoga. He got down
and he did some poses. Really badly. I don't know why he
did that. He had never done it before. Light travels at
186,000 miles per second. My father said. He was still
thinking about light in darkness. Surely you'd feel that
even more than driving in a fast car. Driving in a fast car
down the highway with the windows down. He said.
Surely that would ruffle your hair. Surely you would feel it
on your skin as it shoots past.

We arrived at the venue in the afternoon. There was the same sound guy working there. The same sound guy that Jaco had said was behind the original Xstabeth LP. But of course he was giving nothing away. He acted like he had never met my father before. But then he made a joke. Don't worry. He said. There will be no key janglers. I think my father must have forgotten how he had behaved. Because he didn't even acknowledge it. My father got up onstage. Can you play us a song. The sound guy said. Can you play us a song so we can check our levels. No songs. My father said. Well. Can you just make a sound. The soundman said. My father took his hand and just banged the guitar for a bit. Is that what you will be doing for the show. The soundman said. It's just I want to get the levels right. I'm not saying. My father said. I'd rather not reveal it right now. I mean there were only three of us in the room. What would it matter. But still. Well. Can you try your mic. The soundman said. Ah. My father said. Ah. Into the mic. Is that how you are going to be singing during the show. The soundman said. My father just looked at him. With no expression at all. Okay. The soundman said. I guess we're done. Phew. My father said. That was like pulling teeth. Then he said. Listen. I want the room to be completely dark when I play. I want complete darkness. The people behind the bar are not going to be happy about that. The soundman said. They need to sell drinks. They need light to count the money. For God's sake what does that have to do with art. My father said. What about if they had torches. What if the bar staff had torches to work by. He said. I'm trying my

best to turn this into a total art environment. He said.
Work with me here. The soundman looked at him. And
for a second it was if he acknowledged that my father was
Xstabeth. Or at least her chosen representative. Whatever
you say. He said. After all. It's your show. But you supply
the torches. He said. My father said. I need to be alone. I
need to commune. That's what he said. So I went off to
buy some torches.

When I came back. When I came back my father was
standing on his head in the dressing room. Listen. He
said. Listen. I want you to know that I love you. He said.
Still upside down. I want you to know that. In case
anything happens. What could happen. I asked him. I'm
putting it all on the line here. He said. It's a leap of faith.
He said. Across a chasm. He said. Into the dark. He said.
From a great height. He said. Into the silence. He said.
Why are you upside down. I asked him. I want to hear
the rush of the blood. He said. I want to hear the rush of
the blood. I want you to know that you can do nothing
wrong. He said. What a thing to say to another person.
What a thing for your father to say to you. I felt blessed.
And excited. And upset too. Now go. He said. Now leave
me here. He said.

I went for a walk. I went for a walk in St. Peters. All in
the snow. Which was falling so softly. So delicately. I
looked out at the river. And of course it was frozen. There
were people playing on the ice. Gliding back and forth on
the ice in St. Peters. It seemed so precarious. I didn't dare

go out on it myself. After all. After all I had to see my father's show. Everything had led up to this. I walked some more and I got a little lost. I remember feeling as if someone had rearranged the city. Behind my back. Subtly. Strangely. Where streets connected at odd points. Where squares let out onto new avenues. Where buildings appeared where before there had been none. Where grim old monuments to tragic revolutionaries flitted about like chess pieces. And new bridges. New bridges appeared. New bridges that I didn't dare cross. And of course grim apartments with no heating. Where they had never been before. But that might have been the snow talking. I walked around in a confused dizzy state. I let my baby lead me. That's what I told myself. And then I realised I was outside Jaco's apartment. The one my father and I had stood outside of not so long ago. I had no idea how I got there. I looked up and saw a figure at the window. Was it Jaco. Jaco. I said. I called out through the frozen air. But the figure. The figure who was really just a silhouette. A silhouette on a winter's day in St. Peters with no features. The figure reached up and drew the curtains shut. I thought about ringing the buzzer. About ringing the buzzer and asking for Jaco. Then I realised. I realised it was my baby kicking me. My baby kicking me. Backwards. Into the past. And I resisted it. We had to go forwards. Us two. I knew that now. Besides. Besides you can get into a lot of trouble ringing the wrong buzzer in Russia.

I eventually found the venue but it seemed like it was on

a different street. It was almost buried in snow. And the
windows were frosted over. Inside I saw The Snork. Sat
by an open stove. The light casting shadows on his face. It
looked like a brain. A brain for a face. A red-hot brain.
He looked at me then. He looked at me with a single eye.
From under a fold of flesh. But I don't think he
recognised me. But who knows. Because he smiled. He
smiled like he knew it all. So who knows. The club wasn't
busy. There were about fifteen people sat on stools or
stood around at the bar. Then the young sound guy made
an announcement. By special request of the artist. He
said. I felt so proud of my father right then. The artist.
The artist has requested darkness. He said. Then he killed
the lights. Behind the bar I saw two torches click on. But
that was it.

There was a quiet murmur in the room. Then someone
took the stage. All you could hear in the room was
footsteps. But weird footsteps. Like one foot was heavier
than the other. Or shorter. Clump-CLUMP. Then silence.
Clump- CLUMP. Then there was the sound of water. The
sound of water flowing. Glug-GLUG. Glug-GLUG. The
rivers have thawed. I thought to myself. The rivers have
thawed. Then there was muttering. A voice. Everyone was
straining. To hear what it said. Everyone was rapt.
Someone went to order a beer at the bar. They whispered
to the barman. A shadow in the dark. Everyone turned to
look at him. Suddenly everything was significant. Then
there was the sound of sliding. The sound of sliding and
pulling onstage. You couldn't make out anything. It was

like your eyes would never adjust to the dark. Like inside
the dark it was darker still. And that's where the
performance was taking place. But was it even a
performance. Later someone said it was like a crime
scene. Yes. That was exactly it. It sounded like a body. A
body being dragged across the stage. A body being
displayed in the dark. Then there was silence. Well. Near
silence. Not quite. Something was sitting onstage.
Something had dragged something else onstage. And was
now sitting next to it. It seemed. If you listened. If you
listened you could hear breathing. Breathing somewhere
near a microphone. This lasted about five minutes.
Everyone in the room was afraid to move. Then there was
the smell. A smell began to gather. It smelled like horse
dung. Like something rotting. But positive. If you know
what I mean. Like healthy decay. Like fertiliser. There
were rumours afterwards that whoever it was onstage had
tried to make a bomb. They had tried to make a bomb.
Live in front of an audience. But that it had failed to go
off. After what seemed like eternity itself. After that the
thing onstage. Why do I call it a thing. Wasn't it my
father. I don't know anymore. The thing onstage lit a
cigarette. There was a sudden spark. And people gasped.
People gasped and jumped back. They thought he was
lighting the fuse. People said afterwards. They thought he
was lighting the fuse that would blow us all to kingdom
come. Of course he was. Art should be like a hand
grenade thrown through an open window. At random. Of
course he was. All you could see onstage was the glow of
the cigarette. And as it moved it left patterns in the air.

People claimed it spelled out a word. But no one could agree on what. Someone said it spelled SOS. But to me it was the birds. The birds were back again. The simple birds from my father's journal. Simple shapes. The view from the beach. Always returning. Again and again. Then there was music. Oh God. There was music. But it was like nothing you ever heard. I swear that this thing onstage. Which was my father or whatever it was. This shape began what sounded like blowing. Like blowing over the strings of a guitar. A guitar that it had picked up. And it was rippling. A single chord was rippling. Droning. (E minor.) Droning. (E seventh.) Rising and falling. So delicately. Then it sounded like there was singing. Like there was singing under the breath. Like it was singing to itself. Why do I say it. That's what it seemed like. I have to be honest. If my father was there. If my father was sitting up. Or if my father was dead on the stage. Which was a possibility. It felt like anything was possible. Either way it was like there was no personality. It was an it. A thing. A happening. An event. And it was like the music. The music was a beautiful duet with the moment. That the music was duetting with time. And time was duetting with space. And everything in the room was playing along. Every movement. Every sound. (Droning.) I began to feel an incredible sensation. At the base of my spine. (Droning.) Rising up and rising down. But higher each time. (Droning.) Until it felt like I was gushing. Gushing all over my brain. I almost cried out. I thought I heard someone crying. In the room. I swear. Muffled tears. In the silence. (Droning.) And then the sounds stopped. The light of the cigarette had gone. And there was dead silence. Heart-stopping silence. Everyone was afraid to breathe. No one moved in their chair. It was electric. Everything was heightened. How long did it go on. I don't know. How long did we sit there. Frozen. Sounds from outside the venue began to drift in. Distant voices. A car struggling in the snow. Music from far away. People tiptoed behind the bar. People looked at each other in the dark. Trying to gauge the situation. Trying to read their reactions. Nothing happened. But nothing kept on happening. People began to get restless. Was it all over. Then a woman behind the bar. A woman took a torch and directed it towards the stage. No. People gasped. Don't do it. It was like there was a vampire hidden in the corner. A vampire no one wanted to see. People covered their eyes. Covered their eyes and looked through their fingers. The beam crossed over the ceiling. And fell down towards the stage. And cut through the silence. In an arc. Had this been orchestrated too. Was it all part of the show. And when it came to the stage. When the light hit the stage. There was nothing. There was no one there. There was just a guitar. Laid on a stool. And that's when we heard the ticking. From inside the bag. From inside the bag that the torch lit up. The bag that lay on the stage next to the stool. A black bag. That was ticking. There was panic spreading through the room. No doubt. But no one could move. Everyone was paralysed. Looking at this black ticking bag. In the beam of a torch. On an empty stage. Empty except for a guitar. Suddenly I felt so sad. It was so awful. I remembered the terrible fish.

The terrible fish my father had torn in two. In St. Andrews. I had the same feeling. And I don't know what made me do it. I don't know. But I got up. I got up and walked over to the stage. Someone tried to stop me. They grabbed me by the arm. But then someone else said. Leave her. Leave her. It's the daughter. And they let me go. I walked up to the stage. And I opened the bag. Inside was a clock. An old-fashioned clock. Ticking. I turned around. In the light of the torch. And held it up for the audience to see. And they began to clap. They began to cheer. With relief. I think. It was so sad. Why. It was so awful. That clock in the old plastic bag. Ticking away on its own. I began to cry. I began to cry. And everyone left. Everyone got up and left. The show was over. They thought. The show was over. And they turned on the lights. There was no one there. No one but the young sound guy. Who came over to me. Who came over to me and took the clock from my hands. And led me away. And said this is where the heart ends. This is where the heart ends. He said.

GRACE IN XSTABETH
by Aneliya Andropov

L et us first locate grace in its most common everyday
occurrence. Which would be an extraordinarily
beautiful young girl. Walking as if on water. Let us now
lend her two sisters. Whom we will title Isrobing and
Islence. There you have the classical Graces. As it were
born again. We can see then that grace is something that
is bestowed. And that itself bestows. Grace is revealed as
the perpetual engine of myth and science. Grace is what
Newton and Einstein failed to postulate. Indeed. Grace
seems as impossible as the flight of a bumblebee. Which
it must be admitted isn't necessarily graceful. Grace also
implies a certain thank-you. Who hasn't thanked the stars
and God above at the sight of a beautiful young girl. Her
hair trailing in the wind. Her dainty steps one after the
other in the summertime. To appreciate the gait of a
slender young girl at that time of year is to be gracious.
Grace can also be experienced in the cut of a fine suit. Or
some nice swimming trunks. Perhaps it would be more
correct to say that grace both bestows and diminishes.
Grace removes what is timely. It gifts us with its absence.
Which becomes another form of grace. This is the grace
of ageing. Which is tied in with another word that passes

for an exclamation of perfectly poised beauty. And that word is mercy. We demand mercy of the universe when it looks to overwhelm us with grace. We long to stop the young girls in the street with their long flowing dresses and perfectly proportioned pins and say. No. Please. It is too much my dear. Although the mean of grace is fluctuating its power just like gravity is constant. But to have grace is also to know one's limits. Young girls and old men maintain grace through caring and conversation rather than carousing and complicating. No matter how much the grace of the young girl may unsettle. That is when the cry of mercy reaches the lips. And the conversation is subtly steered towards matters of the weather and the topic of yesterday. Yesterday is a topic that requires grace. In company when it is spoken you can be sure that grace has entered the scene. But grace can also make itself known as a form of disinterestedness. Grace relaxes its grip even as it anoints the calves of young girls in conspiracy with gravity and biology. It tightens as a bodice even as it loosens like an old well-loved couch that has had its day and is grateful. Because grace is something to be grateful for. Old men are particularly thankful for it. You can witness this on the benches of seaside towns where grace itself has brought them. Sometimes initially against their will. It must be said. But that is something we must take up with time itself. Despite time's intimate relationship with grace. Grace comes up behind time and provides both salt and consolation. Here we should recall the story of the man who was hidden from civilisation for decades. On his emergence his first request was for salt. Salt was what he had missed the most. Grace is difficult if not pointless in seclusion. But even there it operates. And it is necessary to have the good grace to accept our situation. But on the whole grace is something that requires observation; hence this book is a requirement of grace. Hence the previous sentence requires a semi-colon. One runs from the other in a way that is delightful. I say good grace because grace is something that we must come to terms with in the long run. I say long run because as I have intimated grace is something that comes with age. I say comes with age because grace is something that makes itself known when we are older. I say also that grace is present in the young as they tumble and fall and get back up again. All with grace. Yet I insist that grace is something that *makes itself known* in age. Grace as I have hinted is something that is gifted. How else would we let go the lovely bodies of our youth. The lovely flawless bodies of our youth with such grace as to surely intimate the working of a heavenly hand. If not for the gift of grace itself. Because as much as it might upset or confuse the reader. Grace also has a hand in the deadening of things. It is said that people go to their deaths with grace. As if they have taken the hands of Isrobing and Islence and retreated across the soft dewy grass with silent footsteps. Then forgetting too becomes a graceful act. Grace descends and the pain becomes lighter. The memory softer. Grace works to soothe feelings and to quell rages. Grace allows us to separate ourselves from everything we believed we once were.

The old man on the bench at the seaside resort. He has taken the passing of the beautiful bodies of his youth with grace. The way you accept a summer shower. He sits there in the shower and he feels the rain fall. From his vantage point above the beach he can see the rain come in. And he can see where it will end. He watches a beautiful young girl untie her loose dress and reveal a white one-piece swimming costume. At one point the sight of a beautiful girl in a swimming costume would have sent uncontrollable feelings of love and longing through his body. Now grace has intervened. Not for me. He thinks. The complications of other bodies. The overstuffed handbags held gracefully halfway up the arm. The words of the floppy summer hat and oversized sunglasses are now muted. They appear as distant birds. He calls her by her name. Grace. He recalls her sisters. Isrobing & Islence. He takes out a pen and a piece of paper. There it is: &